Durable Goods
by
Patricia Hale

Copyright April 2018

All rights reserved. No part of this book shall be reproduced or transmitted in any form or by any means, electronic, mechanical, magnetic, photographic including photocopying, recording or by any information storage and retrieval system, without written permission of the publisher. No patent liability is assumed with respect to the use of the information contained herein. Although every precaution has been taken in the preparation of this book, the publisher and author assume no responsibility for errors or omissions. Neither is any liability assumed for damages resulting from the use of the information contained herein.

This is a work of fiction. Names, characters, places, and incidents either are the product of the author's imagination or are used fictitiously. Any resemblance to actual events or locales or persons, living or dead, is entirely coincidental.

ISBN: 9781940758695 Paperback
ISBN: 9781940758718 EPUB
ISBN 9781940758701 Mobi

Cover Design: Shelley Holmgren

Published by:
Intrigue Publishing, LLC
11505 Cherry Tree Crossing Rd. #148
Cheltenham MD 20623-9998

*In memory of
W. K. Hayes
and for
Marjorie Hayes
with love*

Acknowledgments

My deepest thanks goes out to the many people who are behind this endeavor. The outstanding team at Intrigue Publishing for their expertise and support, I am so grateful to be working with you. Melanie Rigney, my editor, for knowing what works, what doesn't, and catching me when I slip. For my readers, Tina Perry Buckley and Heather Smart who see all the things I don't. Above all, my husband, Mike, and my children Jenny, Jeff and Micah, it's your faith that keeps me at my desk. Lastly, to my constant companions, Enya and Muddy, who wait patiently for their walks until the last word hits the page.

Durable Goods

ORACLES of the KINGDOM

MONDAY

He walked into Bennett's Market looking like anybody else in search of gas and junk food. I was disappointed. I thought he'd stand out, thought he'd be the kind of person that makes you hesitate and forget for a moment what you were doing. But he was any guy, tall, gaunt and unshaven in worn out jeans with a split across one knee that gaped when he walked, like a mouth gasping for air. The sleeves of his faded flannel shirt were rolled to his elbows. I recognized the *Jesus Saves* tattoo on his forearm from the file I'd seen on Isaac Bennett at the St. Bart police station.

He walked toward me and nodded. I slipped a bag of Cheetos beneath my poncho, into the waistband of my pants, and nodded back. A hint of a smile appeared in his eyes.

I glanced at my partner, Griff Cole, standing on the other side of the store, flipping through the pages of *Popular Mechanic*. Griff looked like a tourist in his gray wool sport jacket, jeans and square-toed Buckaroos. This time of year, most Mainers were in their winter uniforms, flannel shirts, down vests and LL Bean boots. A spray of black hair fell over his forehead and he raked it back with his free hand, taking in Bennett. His eyes grazed mine before dropping back to the magazine.

"Cigs," Bennett said to the girl behind the counter nodding to the overhead rack. "And twenty bucks on number 3."

The clerk punched some numbers into the register. "Cigarettes are out back still boxed. I have to go get them, but your gas is all set."

"Back in a minute, then," he said to her.

I stood in front of the candy rack and stuffed a Snickers bar in with the Cheetos, timing it so he'd see me do it as he turned from the counter.

"Hungry?" he whispered with a conspiratorial wink.

I stepped away from him fast and tried to look scared, which wasn't entirely untrue.

"Hey lady, you need help or something?" the clerk asked.

"Just looking," I said.

"Well, hurry it up. This ain't a hangout." She raised her arms over her head, split her ratty ponytail in half between fisted hands and pulled it tight.

"Ahh, leave her alone, Ruth," Bennett said smiling at me. "It's a big decision."

Ruth disappeared in search of his cigarettes and I watched him walk out the door and over to his truck. There was a hitch in his step that suggested, despite his lean frame, he wasn't in his prime. Weathered and early forties, the seat of Bennett's jeans hung low off his bony hips and he looked in need of a meal. Standing alongside his pick-up, he shoved the gas nozzle into the tank of the F-150 and kept his eyes on the storefront.

I looked at Griff again. He nodded.

At the cooler against the wall, I took out an ice tea then reached back in and knocked a bottle of root beer onto the tiled floor. It shattered, creating a bubbling, brown puddle of soda and glass.

Ruth reappeared from the back of the store, holding a carton of Marlboros in her hand. "What the…?" She started toward me.

"I'm sorry," I said. "I'll clean it up. Have you got a mop?" I reached my arm toward her and with my other hand beneath my poncho, released the candy and Cheetos, letting them fall into the puddle at my feet.

Ruth looked at me then at the parking lot where Bennett was fiddling with the gas tank and back to me again. "I'll clean it. You get the hell out of here," she said, her tone more anxious than angry.

"No really…" I started, but she cut me off.

"Get the hell out, now," she said, her eyes shifting toward the door.

The bells above the entrance jingled as Bennett stepped inside. "You mind your mouth," he said pointing a long, nicotine- stained finger at Ruth. "What's going on?"

Her eyes bore into me, conveying something I couldn't discern then she turned toward Bennett. "She's got a bunch of stuff under her shirt and making a friggin' mess too." The irritation was back in her voice.

"I said, watch your mouth." He turned to me. "You really are hungry."

I didn't speak and started to move away from him, but he grabbed my wrist.

"It's okay. You can have those." He bent and lifted my candy and Cheetos out of the puddle of root beer, wiped them on his jeans and handed them back to me. He fished in his pocket, pulled out a five-dollar bill and handed it to Ruth. "That'll cover her food and clean this up."

She took the money, dropped her hand to her side and stood for a moment looking at the floor.

"Mop," Bennett barked.

Without a word, Ruth turned toward the back of the store.

Bennett watched her go then looked at me. "What's your name?"

"Britt."

"You need a ride, Britt? And maybe a meal?"

I nodded.

Before following him out the door, I glanced at Griff one last time. My going undercover to investigate Bennett was an argument Griff had lost. But this case had opportunity written all over it, personal and professional and as usual, I hadn't given up until I got what I wanted. I'd been so fixated on my chance to shine that I'd dismissed the unknowns of the case as insignificant. Like who was Isaac Bennett beyond his rap sheet for disturbing the peace? And what else was for sale at Oracles of the Kingdom besides organic produce? Looking back now, I see that I put glory ahead of common sense and what happened to me was my own fault. I'd been in this too long to make such a rookie mistake.

The door of Bennett's beat to hell pick-up whined as he opened it. "Hop in, sweetheart," he said. His eyes moved from my sneakered feet to my cropped black hair and back.

My heart beat a hole in my chest as I settled on the passenger seat and closed the door. We pulled onto the road, fishtailing through slushy snow left over from last night's storm. I stared straight ahead and tried to breathe, telling myself that I could do this, I really could. At least I was pretty sure that I could.

"You got anyplace to be?" he asked.

I shook my head. "No." My voice cracked and the word came out in a whisper.

"I got somewhere you can rest and get something to eat. Sound good?"

I looked at him and nodded, even tried to smile.

He palmed my head and shook it beneath his hand. "What's with the haircut, you tryin' to pass for a boy?"

"It's easy to take care of."

"Don't think there's much chance of you bein' mistaken for the opposite sex anyway." His eyes fell to my breasts and he gave me a knowing grin.

I loosened my poncho, folded my arms beneath it and turned away from him watching the pine trees sail past. We swerved and skidded over the road, avoiding frost heaves and potholes characteristic of Maine's winter. Griff would be on his way back to Portland by now. Mission accomplished.

"Where were you heading?" he asked with a sidelong glance.

I shrugged. "No place in particular."

"Nobody looking for a pretty girl like you?"

I shook my head and my stomach tightened.

He smiled looking pleased with himself, like he'd just lured a fish into his net.

"Why are you helping me?"

"We're all God's children. I like to help Him out when I can. But don't think of this as a hand out. It's food and a bed in exchange for labor."

I nodded.

"Where you from?"

"Portland."

"What're you doing this far north?"

"My mother lived in Bangor."

"Lived as in not anymore?"

"She died last month."

"Sorry to hear that."

I shrugged. In truth, my mother was probably alone in the shadows of our non-descript colonial, conversing with a bottle of vodka. That is if she hadn't passed out yet. Not that I cared. Dead or incoherent, it was all the same to me.

"Your dad?"

"Don't know him." That was mostly the truth too. My dad spent so much time with his college students (the female ones) that I really didn't know much about him except for what my mother had told me. By her standard, he was a no good son-of-a bitch. At this point in my life I was well beyond caring what he was.

"Friends?"

"I haven't lived anywhere long enough to make any."

"Well you'll make some now." He squeezed my hand.

I forced myself not to pull away. I needed Isaac Bennett to like me because I had something to prove and four days to do it.

THE WEEK BEFORE

It was hard to believe that only a week ago, I'd been snorkeling in the turquoise waters of St. John with my boyfriend and business partner, Griff Cole, and his daughter, Allie. But our wheels had no sooner touched the tarmac on our return flight and Griff's cell phone rang. He'd lifted the phone to his ear.

"John," he said.

"Stark?" I mouthed.

He nodded at me. Agreed to something John said over the phone and hung up.

"Now what?"

"Needs a favor."

"Regarding?"

"Kira. He thinks she might have contacted him."

"We've got a couple of other cases ready to go."

Griff nodded. "I know."

"So…"

"So we fit John into our schedule." He gave me a sideways smile and squeezed my hand. "We'll make it work."

John and Griff's dad were partners on the force. When they walked in on a liquor store robbery after a department softball game, both were off duty. John walked out. Griff's father didn't. John took over as a father figure so when he comes to Griff for help, saying no is not an option.

We were loading our bags into the trunk of a taxi when a black Suburban pulled to the curb behind us. Official CID plates, Portland, Maine's Criminal Investigation Department, told us it was no welcoming party.

Allie looked at Griff. "Dad, you're not going to work already, are you?" She turned to me, her eyes tearing up. "Mom won't be home from the hospital until tomorrow. I thought we'd have tonight to..." Her eyes fell to the pavement then came back up to rest on me. "Just be together."

I put my arm around her shoulders. "Nobody's taking your father away from you. You know him better than that."

"When I said let's talk, I didn't mean at the airport." Griff said to Detective John Stark as he approached from the Suburban. "I thought we might at least unpack first."

John stood in front of us, hands in his pockets. A preemptive snow shower dusted the sleeves of his wool coat. He nodded toward his SUV. "C'mon, you don't need a cab. I'll take you." He stepped past us and lifted Allie's suitcase from the trunk of the taxi.

Griff glanced at me and shrugged. Grabbing the strap of his canvas bag and the handle of my carry-on, he followed John to the back of the idling Suburban.

"Dad," Allie protested with a sidelong glance at John.

"It's just a ride home, Allie," Griff said.

"A ride and dinner," John added.

The aroma of Chinese food, Allie's favorite, hit us as soon as we opened the doors of the vehicle. A hint of a smile crossed her mouth and she gave John a roll of her eyes that said she knew a bribe when she smelled one. Griff slid onto the passenger seat and Allie and I settled in the back, my stomach growling in anticipation.

John eased the car to a stop in front of a brick townhouse in Portland's West End. A downsize for Griff after his divorce from Eliza and a far cry from the lake house they'd owned for seventeen years. Griff said the only thing he missed was the ample stock of bass.

"Get the door," Griff said handing me his keys. "John and I can get the luggage. Allie..."

"I've got it," she said and stepped from the SUV with a take-out bag under each arm.

With the cardboard containers laid out on the counter and a pile of forks and spoons beside them, we filled our plates and sat around the kitchen table.

"Drinks?" Griff asked setting a beer in front of his plate and handing one to John.

"No thanks," John said, holding up his hand. "Water's fine."

Griff hesitated for a second then glanced into his near empty frig. "Coke?"

"Even better," John said keeping his eyes on his plate.

Griff and I exchanged glances. I'd never known John to refuse alcohol in any form. Since the death of his wife three years ago and the subsequent disappearance of his daughter, Kira, he struggled for a reason to get out of bed every day. So the sight of him now refusing a drink was something I'd never seen before.

When stomachs were full, Allie had reluctantly excused herself to take a shower and John tossed a picture of Kira onto the table. Wavy, blond hair, a full grin of straight white teeth and cobalt eyes laughed at us from the photo. She'd been fifteen when Alexis succumbed to cancer and refused to forgive her father for not placing her in the best oncology unit in the country. Two weeks after the funeral she'd disappeared. In the first year of her disappearance she was high priority, but as one year turned to two and then a third without a trace of her, the department backpedaled. They called her a runaway, labeled the case *cold* and shelved it.

John tossed a postcard on top of the picture. It had been torn into tiny pieces and taped back together. It read, "*OK*".

"You think this is from her?" Griff asked.

"It's from her," John said. "I know it."

"You tear it up?"

"Came like that."

Griff raised his eyebrows.

"At first I thought she was telling me that she's all right. Then I did a web search on the St. Bart postmark and came up with a blurb on *Oracles of the Kingdom* or *"OK."*

"What is it?" I asked.

"According to the description on the town's website, it's a religious based, organic farm. To me, you put religious and farm in the same sentence and I call it a cult, at the very least a cover. I think she's there and needs help."

"You been up there yet?"

"Twice. The St. Bart sheriff was less than helpful so I went to the department in the next town over, Fort Kent. They'd heard of the place but didn't know much about it. If the farm is a cover for something else, I figured it was smarter to wait for you to get home and come up with a plan than for me to go barging in alone."

Griff picked up the card and turned it over in his hand. He ran his thumb over the postmark. "St. Bart, Maine. What's that, 300 miles or so? Could she be that close?"

"We're going to find out."

"You show this to anyone in the department?" I asked.

"They had their chance to look for her."

"They couldn't catch a break," Griff reminded him. He slapped the card against the palm of his hand. "This might give them one."

"I'm already on their shit list. If this turns out to be nothing it'll just add fuel to the fire. Screw 'em. I'll pull them in if I need to, but I have to have something solid first." John checked his watch. "I've got to go."

"Where to?"

"A meeting."

"As in AA?" I asked.

He nodded.

"What brought this about?"

He took the postcard from Griff and raised it up. "This did. Tomorrow morning I'll meet you at your office. I don't need the department looking over my shoulder. Let's take a ride to St. Bart, see if the sheriff's a little more friendly with three of us there.

After he closed the door I looked at Griff. "What do you think?"

He shrugged. "It's a place to start. We never had one before."

"Do you think Kira sent it?"

"I don't know, but the answer to that will either keep John on his feet or send him to his knees. He's been in limbo ever since she disappeared. It's time she released him, one way or another.

OK
MONDAY

"Like hell," Griff said when I brought up the idea of infiltrating OK.

"I'm the best shot you have to find out if Kira's there."

"You have no idea what you could be walking into."

"What other option is there? We have no evidence that would call for police involvement at this point and the only way to get it is to get inside. Of the three of us, I'm the one who can do that."

After a considerable amount of arguing, Griff agreed. "You have four days," he said, "then I'm pulling you out, with or without Kira."

So here I was, a little over a week post vacation, in a beat up truck with Isaac Bennett, the founder of *Oracles of the Kingdom*. On my way to a working farm where I would retrieve my soul and get my life back on track by following the teachings of Jesus Christ. The oracles had to be recruited by Isaac, like Jesus selecting His apostles. I was now one of the chosen. My mission was to get in, look for Kira and get out. Four days, piece of cake, right?

We'd driven about twenty minutes when Bennett made a right turn. From what I could tell we were in the Moosehead Lake region, not far from the Canadian Border. At first it looked like he was taking us head-on into a wall of evergreen trees, but just as I raised my arm to shield my face, a path about five feet wide appeared between two Blue Spruce and we continued forward on a logging road.

"How the hell does anyone find this place?" I asked.

"That's the point," Bennett said. "They don't. I decide who comes in, not the other way around. Only those I deem worthy."

"Then I should consider myself lucky."

"Blessed." He said. "I like to think of it as blessed."

I'd worked hard persuading Griff that I could pull this off. But now, rolling down this obscured dirt road beside Bennett, I heard Griff's argument again…"You could end up way out of your league." I wondered if he'd been right.

We left the tree line behind us. The road widened and on either side of us the landscape opened. To my left, a small herd of Scottish Highlands stood pawing in a frozen pasture, hoping to get lucky. On the other side, an untouched layer of snow stretched for acres.

"You can't tell from looking at it, but that field feeds us year round. So do they." He pointed to the cattle still worrying the ground.

"Us?" I asked.

"Those the Lord puts in my path. Like He did you today. He sends me the souls that need taking care of."

"I thought you said you decided who got in."

He looked at me, his eyes narrowed. "We work together, the Lord and I. Did we make a mistake this time?"

The warning in his eyes said I needed to backpedal fast. "I don't think He makes mistakes."

He smiled and nodded. "Nicely put, sister."

We ascended a sharp rise in the road and a faded yellow farmhouse appeared ahead. A few green shudders hung askew and the roof sagged like the shoulders of someone weary of living.

"Is that where the souls live?" I asked.

"Oracles," Bennett said. "We call ourselves Oracles of the Kingdom. The house is where I live and whoever I choose to keep me company, but that must be earned."

Something in his tone made my stomach shift.

"Where do the rest live?" I asked.

He took a left at the end of the pasture and pointed straight ahead. "Home sweet home," he said and winked at me.

He stopped the truck in front of a long low building resembling a dairy barn. Square windows about a foot wide lined the sides of the building, each one covered with iron bars in a tic-tac-toe pattern.

"Go on in. Find yourself a bed. The women will be coming back soon for lunch."

I stepped out of the truck and reached for my backpack, but his hand was on it. "I'll keep this," he said.

Griff and I had planned for that and put only a change of clothes, a toothbrush, toothpaste and a dummy cell phone inside. The other one was strapped snuggly against my thigh. "My stuff's in there. It's all I have."

He shook his head while rifling through the bag. His hand came out with the cell phone tight in his grasp and a smile on his face. "Everything you need is here." He gestured toward the building and pasture. "All you have to do is what I ask of you in Jesus' name and you'll want for nothing."

I stepped back from the truck and watched him pull away remembering Griff's parting words. "I don't like sending you down the rabbit hole alone," he'd said.

Something told me I'd just landed.

The dormitory building held two rows of bunk beds, fifteen deep. Army style. Each bed was perfectly made, corners tucked and quarter ready. I flashed on my own double bed at home, rumpled blankets strewn with clothes in small heaps. There was one bedroom built into the corner of the room, closest to the door. It was Amish plain. One lone twin bed, a dresser and a nightstand were the only furniture, a lamp and a Bible, the only accessories. I walked down the center aisle of the barracks. The foot of each bed held a name sign, but none said Kira. The last set of bunks on the right side of the rectangular room had no name. I climbed onto the top one.

I'd stashed the picture of Kira that John had given me underneath the insole of my shoe. I slipped it out now to memorize the face of a girl I'd met a handful of times and hadn't seen in three years.

I unfastened the cell phone from my thigh, got up and walked around the dormitory hoping for at least one bar. In the tiny, closet sized bathroom I got what I needed and texted Griff.

I'm in. Turnoff on right 10 minutes @ 50 mph from market. Dirt path btwn 2 Blue Spruce. 1st bldg women's dorm. cafeteria and barn on right. House straight ahead.

We'd agreed on no in-coming calls under any circumstance. I would call out only if I had to, otherwise any messages would be sent by text and the fewer words the better. He needed the layout of the property so he'd know where to find me when the time came.

The bathroom was relatively clean, obviously somebody's daily job. Maybe I could make it mine since that was the only place with reception. There were two pedestal sinks side by side, each with green watermarks around the drain. One toilet to my right and two shower stalls beyond, both had clear, glass doors instead of curtains. No privacy. I felt around the pine floor for anything loose where I could hide the phone. No dice. Above me there was a light fixture and a grate for a ceiling fan that didn't work. With one foot on the bathtub and one on the sink, I pried open the grate. Dust mites fell on my face and my fingertips slid over greasy residue, but that was all good. It meant no one bothered to clean the grate. I placed the photo of Kira and my cell inside and screwed it back in place. Back in the main room, I climbed onto the top bunk and waited for what would come next.

The door opened jingling the chimes hanging above it, a rudimentary alarm. I sat up startled and jumped off my bed to see who'd come in. Ruth, the clerk from Bennett's Market was closing the door behind her. I stepped into the center aisle. She looked at me for a moment as though trying to remember where she'd seen me before.

"Sorry about the mess," I said.

She shrugged and walked toward the small bedroom, nylon wind pants swishing between her ample thighs.

"How long have you lived here?" I asked.

"All my life. Isaac's my father."

I tried not to show my surprise. "Your mother live here too?" I asked. Ruth's blocky build hadn't come from him.

She looked at me acknowledging the question, but didn't answer. She bent forward and untied her work boots. The leather was dark from the damp ground outside. A couple of decaying leaves clung to the soles.

"How come you don't live in the house?" I asked.

"I live here with the workers to provide leadership. You're my responsibility."

"Leadership for what?"

"It would be in your best interest not to ask so many questions. Be grateful that you've been taken from the masses and handpicked to be one of us. There's no higher calling." She sounded like a recording, no affect, just repetition. She disappeared inside the bedroom and closed the door.

The barracks' door opened and again the bells, annoying as all hell, sounded the alarm. Ruth was immediately in her doorway.

About thirty women filed in, their ages ranging from fifteen to forty, at a guess. At thirty-three, I was one of the elders. Though I still got carded in most bars, I wondered if age would hurt my chances of getting into Isaac's house. The women were all dressed exactly the same in jeans, blue sweatshirts and work boots. Ruth nodded as each woman passed and they returned the gesture before seeking out their individual bunk. Home sweet home.

Almost in unison, they lay on their beds, removed a Bible from under their pillows and began to read. I followed suit, feeling under my pillow and finding my own. The room was eerily silent. Satisfied, Ruth went back into her bedroom and closed the door.

After a few minutes one woman got up and began making her way to the bathroom. Ruth's door flew open, banging against the wall behind it.

"What're you doing?" She asked.

The woman twirled around to face Ruth, obviously shaken. "I have to use the bathroom."

Ruth glanced at her watch. "Fifteen minutes. Get back in bed."

"But, I have to…"

"Fifteen minutes," Ruth said. "Move it."

The woman returned to her bed. Satisfied, Ruth closed her door.

At twelve-thirty, Ruth appeared again and the women began going into the bathroom in twos. When each pair came out they left the barracks. Ruth approached my bed. I set down my Bible and looked at her.

"Lunchtime," she said. "Wash up and put these on." She handed me a sweatshirt and jeans. "Then come to the cafeteria. Walk up the driveway. It's on the right. You'll see it." She nodded to my watch, a gift from Griff. "I'll take that."

"No," I said. "You can't have this."

"You have no need to know the time here. I'll tell you what to do and when."

"It was a gift from my mother. She passed away recently."

"Material goods are unimportant. What is important is what we carry within us." Ruth nodded again at the watch and held out an open palm.

I placed the watch in her hand. "Will I get it back when I leave?"

She smiled. "Wash your hands and go to lunch."

"Can I ask you one more thing?"

She looked at me and waited.

"Where are the men?"

"What men?"

"Don't you need men for the cattle? For butchering?"

"The cattle are sent out for slaughter. Occasionally Isaac hires day laborers to work the farmers' markets in the summer."

"The women don't go to market?"

Ruth shook her head. "The women don't leave the farm. They are here to put their lives back on track."

"And what happens once they've done that?"

"They repay him for his generosity and love."

"How?"

She nodded toward the door. "You're going to be late. Isaac doesn't like it if you're late."

GRIFF

Griff approached his SUV parked to the rear of Bennett's Market, pulled open the door and slipped onto the driver's seat.

"How'd it go?" John asked.

"No hitches." Griff started the car then pulled out his phone and looked at it.

"She's not going to have a chance this soon."

"Just checking."

"Let's pay Stebbins another visit," John said. "Maybe he'll feel like talking today."

"You gonna tell him about Kira this time?"

"I think I have to. He was so evasive about Bennett before that I held back. Small towns this far north are like one big incestuous family. Everyone's got each other's backs. I was hoping not to tip our hand until we knew where Stebbins' loyalties lie. Don't think I have a choice now. We need him. But I don't want him to know Britt's inside."

They drove the two miles to the St. Bart Police Department over slushy, pitted asphalt long in need of repair.

"Maine infrastructure," John said breaking the silence. "Love it or leave it."

Griff pulled into the PD parking lot and cut the engine. He took out his cell phone and checked it again.

"You're gonna drive yourself crazy looking at it every five minutes."

He slipped it back inside his jacket pocket without answering.

When they'd visited Stebbins with Britt three days ago the sheriff confirmed that Bennett owned Oracles of the

Kingdom as well as the local convenience store, Bennett's Market and shown them a one-page file. Nothing more than a mug shot and a brief report on disorderly conduct then brushed them off saying he had an appointment elsewhere and didn't have time to talk. Today, Stebbins was seated at his desk when they entered. He stood and extended his hand to Griff. "Where's your pretty little partner?"

"Busy," Griff said.

John stepped forward. "Like we told you the other day, Sheriff, we're looking for information on *Oracles of the Kingdom*."

Stebbins shook his head, looked down and studied his desk. "Not much to tell. It's a working farm. Organic. Religious. 'Bout a hundred acres or so, run by a bunch of tree hugging women." He looked up and laughed. "Bennett owns that and the market. Why all the interest?"

John shrugged. "I'm looking for someone. Thought it might be a possibility. Just women? There's more to farming than sowing seeds and baking pies, isn't there?"

That drew another laugh from Stebbins.

"What about the sweat and heavy machinery? Where does Bennett get the muscle?" John asked.

"Hires migrants on occasion," Stebbins said. "Least he used to, not sure if he still does. I don't see much of the guy. Bennett mostly keeps to himself. Sells produce and meat at his store and at the local farmers' market in summer. Harvests maple syrup in the springtime, Christmas trees in the fall, seems to do all right."

"We think there might be more going on there than you're aware of Sheriff," John said.

Stebbins smile faded. "What're you gettin' at, Detective?"

"Just what I said. "I'm not sure you have all the information about what Bennett's doing in there."

"Look," Stebbins' folded his arms across his chest. "I went in there and talked with Bennett about a year ago when some farmers abutting his land started calling him crazy. I wandered around the place. Everything seemed legit, just a workin' farm. Got himself a bunkhouse for the women. It's clean. A barn and a kitchen, nothin' aroused my suspicion that the place ain't what it claims to be."

"Did you speak with any of the women?" Griff asked.

Stebbins scratched his head. "You folks live a different life style down there in the big city. Up here, you don't just walk onto someone's property 'cause it smells funny. People in St. Bart live here because they value their privacy and it's my job to respect and protect. So Bennett might be a little odd. Thinks he's God's right hand man and all, but I can't arrest him for that. Just cause a guy's nuts, don't make grounds for a warrant."

"You got directions to the place?" John asked.

"You got a warrant?"

John took a step back. "I'm just asking where the farm is. I'm not saying we're going in."

"It's up the road a ways. And that's all I'm sayin'. Around here, you go snoopin' onto someone's property you're likely to get your head blown off. And rightly so," he added.

John took a deep breath blew it out and looked Stebbins in the eye. "My daughter's missing," he said. "I have reason to believe she might be on Bennett's farm."

Stebbins' jaw twitched and he kept his gaze on John like he was sizing him up. He sniffed. "Got a picture?"

John took one from his wallet and handed it to Stebbins. While he studied it, his shit-eating grin stalled out. His eyes shifted from John to Griff then back to Kira's smiling face. "You let me go talk to Bennett," he said. "Some out of town cops come in he'll get anxious. He knows me well enough. I'll go see if he knows anything about your daughter."

John nodded. "Appreciate it." He handed Stebbins his card. "I'll be in touch."

"You headin' back to the city?" Stebbins asked.

"For now."

"What'd you think?" Griff asked once they were back in the SUV.

"I don't like him. Too much of a smartass."

"He lost his grin pretty fast when you handed him the picture."

"Yeah, I noticed. Makes me wonder what Stebbins knows and what he's not telling us.

Two hours later on the drive back to Portland John's phone rang. He ended the call after few words and turned to Griff. "Stebbins said Bennett's never seen Kira. Said he'd keep her picture on his bulletin board in case she ever wanders through."

"He didn't waste any time getting in touch with Bennett," Griff said. "What'd you make of that?"

"Not sure. But I doubt his hurry was for our benefit.

"You think he's warning Bennett?"

"Could be."

Griff checked his cell phone. "She's in," he said.

OK
MONDAY

The dining hall was a long low structure attached to the barn like an afterthought. It was set up cafeteria style and I took my place in line with the others. A skimpy, mid-winter salad was followed up with macaroni and cheese, hot dogs and chocolate chip cookies. Servers behind the aluminum tables scooped ample portions onto our plates. Evidently, the help didn't qualify for the farm's organic cuisine, but my Cheetos and Snickers had worn off long ago and my stomach said feed me.

"Heard that." The woman in front of me turned and smiled.

"Guess I'm a little hungry."

"You're new?"

"This morning," I said, looking into a face that was strikingly beautiful. Glancing around the room there wasn't an ugly one among us. Lucky for Isaac, God sure knows how to pick 'em.

"Welcome. I'm Sarah." She pushed a strand of unruly auburn hair behind one ear.

"Britt," I said,

She smiled. "That will change."

"What?"

"Your name."

We'd reached the end of the serving line and I followed her to a table.

"Can I sit with you?" I asked.

"Of course." She slid further down the bench and folded her hands together.

I sat and before doing anything else, shoveled a spoonful of macaroni into my mouth."

"Oh," she said, her eyes wide.

"What?" I said.

"We haven't given thanks yet."

I lowered my head feigning shame.

She touched my hand. "It's okay, you're new. We have to give thanks before eating."

I kept my head down breathing in the aroma of fat and carbohydrates. If that's all I could get for now, I'd take it.

Isaac appeared at the other end of the room and cleared his throat. "Thank you Father," he said, voice booming, body rigid, his arms reaching toward heaven. "Guide my hands that I may shape my followers to your design. Make us worthy of this food we are about to eat and all the goodness you have bestowed upon us." He lowered his arms and gazed from one face to another around the room. "And you, let your gratitude overflow, for without this community you would be just another sinner among the millions."

A loud *Amen* came from the rest of the room.

"Okay," Sarah said to me. "Now you can eat."

I lowered my head and dug in. At first, I couldn't stop eating long enough to start a conversation. When my stomach began to fill, I looked up. "What did you mean when you said my name will change?"

"Isaac renames all of us when we come. We are all named after biblical figures."

"What was your real name?"

She shook her head. "Once we are renamed, our birth name is forever forgotten. We are never allowed to use it again."

"Allowed? What do you mean, allowed?"

"Isaac provides us with everything we need and in return we do as he asks. It's a small request to change our name."

"But it's your identity. It's who you are."

She smiled. "God knows who I am."

My stomach rolled over for the second time that day. "How long have you lived here?" I asked.

"Let's see." She tipped her head to one side, eyes unfocused. "I've been here for three tree pruning seasons." She smiled. "It's hard to keep track, but I know that I was twenty-two when Isaac found me."

"Found you?"

She seemed reluctant to explain, but finally said, "I was a prostitute. It was raining. I was standing under an awning on a street corner in Lewiston. He pulled over, rolled down his window and told me to get in. I'd only had two other tricks that night. It was slow and I hadn't made my quota. I would have been in trouble."

"With your pimp?"

She nodded.

"So what happened?"

"He was very kind. He was gentle." She looked up from her plate and met my eyes. "That wasn't always the case. Afterwards, he told me about *Oracles of the Kingdom.* He said he would take me there if I wanted to go."

"Afterwards? He had sex with you first?"

"I was a prostitute."

"That doesn't mean he had to have sex with you. He could have just offered to help you."

"I was happy to do something for him. He promised to take care of me and said I could live with him forever. I just had to obey his rules and praise God and I would know love like I'd never known it before." She smiled. "How could any girl say no to that?"

I finished my meal in silence.

When women began carrying their empty dishes to a stainless-steel counter on one side of the room, I followed suit and tossed my silverware along with theirs into a gray plastic bucket. Trays were stacked on a wooden table near the door. As each person returned to their seat they knelt on the floor in front of their chair.

Isaac stood at the head of the room waiting for all to kneel. Lowering to my knees, I glanced at the people around me, looking for anyone who had even a slight resemblance to Kira. No one stood out.

With his palm, Isaac flattened greasy, black hair behind one ear. It fell back over his face in defiance. Stroking a straggly beard, he searched the floor for words then raised his eyes.

"Bow your heads, sinners," he said. "Winter cold has made idle hands and I have heard and seen things that displease me. Someone among you knows of what I speak. The rules within the kingdom must be followed." He pounded a fist on the table in front of him. "There is no outside contact. Everything you need is here and will be given to you. Lust is the devil at work. Control is the gift of God. I took you in when you were hungry and fed you. When you were thirsty, I gave you drink. You were naked and I clothed you. You were weak and filthy and pathetic and I have given you the opportunity to be reborn into something worthwhile and beautiful to praise God. If you betray me, you will be subjected to the penance I choose. Scorn me and know my wrath. Obey me and know my love. God has given you free will. Choose your path wisely."

He turned and walked out of the building. Beside me, Sarah was crying. "Return to your beds." It was Ruth speaking. She'd slipped in when Isaac left. "You have one hour to read your Bibles and then back to work." She opened the door and stepped outside.

I caught up with Sarah as she crossed the field to the dormitory. "What was that about?" I asked.

She shook her head and didn't speak.

"How am I supposed to know what I can and can't do if no one tells me?"

"No leaving. No sex. You heard it from Isaac."

"What happens if I don't obey?"

She stopped and looked at me then glanced toward the dormitory where Ruth was standing beside the door. She looked back and hesitated. "Just obey. Do everything he says, that's all you need to know."

She started to turn away and I grabbed her arm. "Are you afraid of him? Why don't you leave?"

"Leave?" She seemed astonished by the idea. "This farm is all I have. Without Isaac and these fields," she waved a hand toward the pasture, "I'd be on the street again. Why would I leave?"

"Hey, you two, let's go," Ruth called from her post.

Sarah hurried toward her glancing back at me just once, fear prominent in her eyes.

I stopped at the door and looked at Ruth. "What happens now?"

"Bible until one-thirty then back to the field."

"The field?"

"They're pruning trees for Christmas."

"What about you?"

She looked unsure about giving me an answer. Giving in she said, "I re-open the store in the afternoon."

I lay on my bed and studied the ceiling. Kira was not living in the dormitory nor had I seen her at lunch. If she was here at all, she was in the house and the only way to know was to get inside. I could sneak in and risk getting caught or I could earn it like Isaac said.

I was close to stir crazy waiting for our one hour of Bible reading to come to an end when the door flew open with a force that sent it bouncing against the wall. Isaac took four long strides down the center aisle and stopped beside Sarah's bunk.

"Get up," he said reaching for her. He grabbed her by the wrist and pulled her from the bed. Her Bible fell to the floor. He kicked it aside.

"I'm sorry," she said. "I'm sorry."

Without answering he dragged her down the aisle. Ruth stood in the doorway of her bedroom. All eyes followed Sarah and Isaac out the door.

"Get out here all of you," Isaac called. "Bear witness to the wrath of the Lord."

In unison, we slipped from our beds and followed one another outside. A fire leapt skyward from the stone pit outside the dormitory.

Isaac held onto Sarah's wrist and pulled her in close to the fire. "This woman betrayed me. She laughed in the face of our Father by ignoring the rules of the kingdom. She will know the fires of hell in this life and if she does not repent she will know them in the next as well."

He slid his grasp upwards around Sarah's elbow and forced her hand into the flames, ignoring her screams as they pierced the frigid air. Tears streamed down her cheeks, her eyes bulged from their sockets and her mouth contorted in pain. The women around me raised their hands to cover their noses and mouths. They stood still and silent. No one made a move to help her. I held my breath against the stench of cooking flesh and took a step forward. Someone grabbed the back of my sweatshirt. It was Ruth, her eyes glowering, warning me not to move. When Isaac finally let go of Sarah's arm she dropped to her knees, wavered and collapsed onto her side clutching the burnt limb to her chest.

"Let that be a lesson to all of you. You will know damnation here on earth and on this farm long before you know it in the afterlife if you fail to heed His word." With that he turned on his heel and walked away. "Clean her up," he said to Ruth as he passed. "The rest of you get to the fields. There's work to be done."

The women turned away, their faces pale and drawn. They walked toward the barn without so much as a whisper among them. I went to Sarah and knelt beside her. Ruth was examining what minutes ago had been Sarah's hand, but was now a bright red stump of curdled blistering skin fused into one claw-like digit.

"Jesus," I said.

Sarah moaned.

"Help me get her inside," Ruth said.

Together we carried her into the dorm and laid her on her bed. Ruth pulled out a cell phone.

"Who are you calling?" I asked.

"The doctor, who do you think?"

"Isaac will allow a doctor to come here?"

"He's a friend. He comes when we need him."

"He'll have to report this. It's abuse."

Ruth sneered. "I said he's a friend of Isaac's. He does what Isaac tells him to. And you better get out to the field. I can handle this."

"But…"

Ruth nodded toward the door. "Go."

I left Ruth with Sarah and went out the door. I hadn't realized how badly my legs were shaking until now. I stopped and leaned against the dormitory and took a breath, closing my eyes. What in hell had she done to deserve that? Why did these women stay? Living on the street was foreign to me. But how could they believe *Oracles of the Kingdom* was a step up? From what I remembered of Kira, she was smart and confident. If she'd had the nerve to defy her father and run away at fifteen, I couldn't see her submitting to Bennett's control. Kira wasn't on the farm. If she was here she was in the house. So no matter how terrified I felt of Bennett right now I had to get inside before I could turn tail and run.

"What the hell are you doing out here?" Ruth let the door fall behind her and stood staring at me. "I told you to get over to the barn."

I stepped away from the dormitory. "I know, I'm going.. I just, I was just…" I stopped and turned back toward her. "What the hell is wrong with him? How could he do that?"

She looked at the ground and shook her head. "He does a lot of things you might not like. Best if you just get used to it. You're not going anywhere."

I kept my mouth shut. Now wasn't the time to argue with Ruth. I turned and headed for the barn. She was a piece of work. She seemed to thrive on her status as our overseer and yet there was compassion beneath her dissonance. And just now, her voice had bordered on kindness. I wondered what demons she lived with as Isaac's offspring and if the hand she'd been dealt was reason enough to want revenge? She was the only one allowed to leave the farm. If Kira was here and had gotten that postcard out, Ruth may very well have been the conduit.

I could see the others ahead of me moving toward the barn. It was like nothing I'd seen before, a colony of women each one walking alone, not in groups of twos or threes, no joking or laughing. Not like the women I knew. These were obedient wives, or worse, frightened children.

"What now?" I asked coming up beside one of the women.

"Chores," she said. "We're pruning. We'll begin cutting and selling in another week. For now we prune every day after breakfast, after lunch, after prayers." She smiled again.

Inside the barn, we each retrieved a pair of tree shears and a small wagon to carry the cuttings. Another group of women would shape the pine branches into circles, adorn some pine cones and a red ribbon and, voila, wreathes. I followed the pruning crew across the field to the trees beyond and like the others, I kept my distance, but once at the tree line I stepped up to a Blue Spruce where the woman I'd spoken to was now cutting boughs.

"Why's everyone always so quiet?" I asked, keeping my voice low.

She glanced at me. "Isaac requests that we work in silence. It allows us to focus on our tasks so we accomplish more. If we must speak then we are to speak to God."

"I don't think He'd recognize my voice," I said and laughed. Two women turned to look at me, each with the same irritated expression.

The woman stepped back taking in the tree that stood before her from top to bottom with an artist's tilt of the head.

I took a step back, copying her move, feeling a bit like a grade-schooler sneaking a peak at the kid's paper beside me. I had no idea what I was looking for. My level of competence when it comes to art is stick figures and I haven't quite mastered them yet.

"Has that ever happened before? I mean what Isaac just did?"

She didn't answer.

"How can you stay here?" I whispered. "He's crazy."

She looked at me and let out a long sigh. "He takes care of us if we follow the rules. It was Sarah's choice to disobey."

"But you're adults. Why do you put up with that?"

She snipped a branch and let it fall to her feet.

"Don't you miss your old life?"

She considered the question for a moment and shook her head. "I'm cared for and I have what I need. My life was miserable before this. I'd go days without food. I was eating out of Dumpsters. How could I miss that?"

"How did you end up like that?"

She glanced over her shoulder. "We shouldn't be talking. He doesn't like it."

"Well, somebody's got to talk to me. How else will I know what's expected? Or even why I'm here? I was hungry. He said he'd give me something to eat. But I wasn't looking for this." I waved my arm toward the surrounding trees.

She stepped away and started trimming branches. I did the same. After a couple of minutes she took a step closer. "Drugs," she said. "The state took my children away. I lost my job and my home. I had nothing until Isaac found me."

"Where was that?"

"In line outside a homeless shelter. He stopped beside me and said he could give me a place to sleep. I got in his truck."

"And he brought you here."

She nodded. "I've never regretted it."

"What about your kids?"

"They're with a foster family somewhere, I suppose."

"Don't you miss them?"

"I never really wanted them, they just sort of happened. Here, I'm clean, no more drugs, I have food, a bed and a purpose."

"A purpose?"

She started to say something, but froze.

"What's all the discussion?" Isaac was suddenly beside me or rather his horse was, a monstrous, black animal pawing the ground and snorting mucous into my hair.

"Jesus," I said and immediately regretted my choice of words.

Isaac made a clicking sound with his mouth and the horse took a step closer, his ironclad hoof coming down on my foot. I screamed, throwing my shoulder into the animal trying to push him off, but it was like butting a stone wall. I was sure I could feel the tiny bones in my foot snapping under his weight.

"Get him off," I yelled at Isaac who grinned down at me.

He backed up the animal and swung his leg over the saddle descending from his perch. One spur-clad boot landed beside my foot. "Sorry," he said. "But Job didn't like what he heard." He nodded toward the horse, his face so close I tasted his breath. "Language like that is not tolerated. The only reason I'll forgo punishment is because you have only just arrived. This moment marks the end of your probationary period."

"Forgo punishment?" I looked down at my foot. The spikes on Job's winter shoe had torn the thin leather of my boot and I was sure my skin beneath it looked just as mangled. "You call that forgoing punishment?"

He stared at me, his eyes dark as river stones.

I thought I was here because you wanted to help me?"

"First, you have to prove yourself worthy."

"And if...?"

The woman beside me squeezed my hand. I lowered my eyes and clenched my teeth pissed, but knowing she was right. I had to back down. "It won't happen again," I said.

Without answering, Isaac climbed onto Job, laid the reins across his neck and spun him in the opposite direction, the horse's coarse, black tail switching across my face. "Get those cuttings back to the barn," he called over his shoulder.

By the time we left the trees my foot was throbbing and swollen. It would only get worse when I took off my boot and the swelling expanded. I limped across the field, pulling my wagon full of mismatched fir behind me. No one offered to help or even acknowledged my difficulty. How great could their fear be that they even refused to take care of each other?

We carried the branches into the barn. I hobbled among them like the hunchback of Notre Dame. By the time I'd delivered all of my greens, returned my wagon to its stall and inched my way back to the cafeteria for dinner, I was too nauseous to eat. I collapsed onto a bench. Someone slid a bowl of chicken soup in front of me as they passed, but I was too consumed by pain to look up to see who it was.

"Eat," the woman beside me said.

"I can't, I don't think it'll stay down. My foot is killing me. I think he broke something."

"You're walking. If something broke, it's only small bones. You'll be fine."

"Thanks for the vote of confidence." I reached for the spoon. Ruth led the prayer of thanks. "Where's Isaac?" I asked between spoonfuls. "I thought he did the prayers around here."

"Ruth keeps watch when Isaac's away."

"Away?"

"In town or at the store."

"Keeps watch?"

She rolled her eyes. "It's just a figure of speech. She's in charge when Isaac's busy."

We ate in silence with the exception of a slurp here and there. Just before we'd finished eating Isaac came into the dining hall and surveyed the room. His eyes came to rest on me. I lowered my head and stared into my soup like a kid afraid to be called on in class. But even without looking, I felt his eyes boring into me and then I saw his feet alongside my own. I looked up.

"I trust we've moved beyond our conversation in the field today?"

I nodded.

"I have given you a gift by bringing you here. I expect gratitude, compliance and respect."

I nodded. His feet moved out of view.

As soon as we were back inside the dormitory, I went to Sarah. She lay staring at the ceiling but turned her head slightly when I knelt beside her. Her hand was wrapped in white gauze and lay on her chest.

"How are you?" I asked.

A tear escaped from the corner of her eye and rolled into her hair. "The doctor gave me some pills. They're helping."

"What was that about?"

"I disobeyed," she said. "It was my penance."

"Burning your hand is penance? Whatever happened to three Hail Mary's and an Our Father?"

"It was to acquaint me with the fires of hell. So that I should know God's will if I continued down that path."

"What could you have done to deserve that?"

"I had sex with a migrant worker."

"What? When? I haven't seen any men since I got here."

"He was here a few days ago meeting with Isaac. He runs a team of migrants. Isaac calls him when he needs work done."

"So you've met him before?"

"It wasn't a one-time thing if that's what you're asking."

"And you got caught."

Sarah nodded. "Isaac has given us everything and I betrayed him. I went against his rule. I can stay and be taken care of, but I will never be chosen."

"Chosen for what?"

"To live with him in the house. When he takes us we are no longer farm hands, we become his, his…"

"His what?"

She shrugged. "I'm not sure, but the women he takes live in his house. They're no longer farm workers. They have a better life than the rest of us.

"You don't know what goes on in the house. It could be worse than working in the fields."

"What's worse than working in a snow covered field in the middle of December with frostbitten fingers and toes? They have a real house, not a dormitory and they spend their days in the comfort of their home, like a wife."

"Polygamy isn't legal."

"It's not polygamy. It's a commitment to love and honor him."

"That's stretching the definition a bit don't you think?"

"Call it what you want. I'll be faithful to him now, but it's too late for me. I will never see the inside of his house."

"What makes you think the women he takes have it so good?"

"It's what he tells us." She shrugged and looked away.

"How can you believe him with no proof? Where are the women now? What do they do in the house all day?"

"I don't know." Her voice rose and we both instinctively looked for Ruth. "We don't see them again. They never come back."

"But you're frightened of him. Why would you want to live with him?"

"He's only cruel if you disobey. Hasn't he fed you since you've been here? Haven't you slept in a warm bed?"

I started to tell her that the food and bed I had at home made this look like a homeless shelter, but I was supposed to be down on my luck. "He almost broke my foot today in the field. That's an odd way to show me he cares."

"Are you all right?" She looked genuinely concerned.

My foot was throbbing, but I nodded. She had enough to deal with without worrying about me.

"He has to have control. He does what he needs to make us worthy."

"Of him or God? Seems like to Isaac they're one and the same."

She didn't answer. Her face was drawn. "Get some sleep," I said. "I'll see you in the morning."

"No, wait." She gripped my forearm with her good hand. "You need to understand. I deserved what he did today. A hand is a small price to pay for food and shelter and love."

"So you forgive him for burning your hand and call it love." I couldn't keep the disgust off my face.

"All of us were addicts, prostitutes or runaways when Isaac took us in. He gave us a home and clothes and food and in exchange we work on the farm and obey his rules. To me that's love."

It was a hard summary to argue, but in actuality it was a pile of brainwashing bullshit. Isaac was picking the most despondent women off the streets for free labor and, I assumed, sex once they were in his house. A monster disguised as the angel of God.

"Why are you risking talking to me now? Why tell me all this?"

She glanced toward Ruth and ducked her head. "You need to know the rules and Isaac tends to teach them by force." She nodded toward my foot." I understand and accept his motives though I may not always agree with his tactics. Now go to sleep."

I walked away from Sarah and stood at the side of my bed devising a plan to get onto the top bunk with a bum foot.

Ruth appeared beside me. "You need a leg up?" she asked.

"Thanks, I'll manage." I dragged myself by the metal sidebar up and onto my blanket.

She took the pillow off the bottom bunk and slipped it beneath my foot. "Keep it elevated," she said then laid three white pills in my palm. "For pain. Lights out in five." She moved away from me, her voice back in drill sergeant mode. "Hurry it up in the bathroom, ladies."

I watched her walk past the other women, go into her bedroom and close the door. A sound outside shook me from my thoughts and I leaned toward the window. Isaac's pickup was moving slowly down the road, its headlights bouncing off the trees. There were shapes in the truck bed, but I couldn't make them out. Machinery or bales of hay, I strained to make out the images, my eyes burning. The truck rolled over the bumpy road, its cargo swaying with the movement. And then in the darkness there was a sudden light, the glow of a cigarette and then another.

"What're you lookin' at?" Ruth was beside my bed, staring up at me.

"Where's Isaac going?"

She glanced out the window. The truck was barely discernable in the distance. "He's making a delivery."

"What's he delivering?"

She tapped her foot against the wooden floor. "He's driving the migrant workers home."

"Migrant workers? I didn't see any workers here today. Where were they?"

"You know your mouth is gonna get you in trouble one of these days."

I couldn't help but smile. "It already has. Countless times."

"Go to sleep," she said and walked down the aisle to her room, closing the door behind her.

I lay back against the pillow and stared at the ceiling considering Isaac's cargo. Migrant workers my ass. I closed my eyes, saw the glow of cigarettes that had come from the truck and thought about how good a Honey Berry cigar would taste right now. Just the thought of that sweetness made my mouth water. I pushed aside my craving and asked myself the question again. Who the hell was in that truck? And how could I find out?

OK
TUESDAY

There were no curtains on the dormitory windows and daylight woke me as soon as it made an appearance. I listened to the sounds of the women, soft snores and deep, relaxed breathing. Outside, a cacophony of birds greeted the new day. Contradictory to what I knew or believed about Isaac's kingdom, I felt peaceful and safe beneath the gray, wool army blanket and almost understood how this place could become a refuge for women who'd been homeless, addicted or abused. But what I couldn't understand is what made them stay once they were back on their feet. Or once they'd witnessed the violence Isaac was capable of.

Ruth's door was closed. Without my watch I couldn't be sure of the time, but sunrise in November hits between six-thirty and seven. I might have a few minutes to get a text off to Griff. I slid off my bed, careful to land on my left foot and stood for a moment listening. No one stirred. Placing my right foot on the worn, pine floor I shifted my weight and tested it out. It was painful, but better. A night's rest and whatever those white pills were had made a difference.

In the bathroom, I hovered above the floor with one foot on the tub and the other on the sink, wincing as I evened out my weight. Loosening the grate overhead, I felt for my cell phone then sat on the toilet and texted Griff.

Bennett crazy. Women for work and sex (I think). Don't worry, just working:) No Kira yet. Inside house? Will text asap. Xo

It wasn't much, but it was all I had for now and at least he'd know I was all right. I slipped the phone back inside the grate, but took the picture of Kira and stuffed it into my sock. I'd show it to Sarah today.

I crept out of the bathroom hoping to make it back to bed before Ruth opened her door and raked her hand through those f-in chimes. No luck.

"What the fuck are you doing?" She stood arms folded, dead center in the aisle between the beds.

"Do you ever sleep?" I asked.

"Answer my question," she said.

"I had to pee."

I could see in her face that she wasn't convinced.

Around us women were lifting their heads, watching.

Ruth kept her eyes on mine. I met them and held on. She dropped her gaze and turned around. "Let's go ladies," she said. "Rise and shine. The trees are waiting."

Like obedient children twenty-eight blankets flipped back, exposing the bodies beneath. Women lined up in twos down the center aisle. Many held their Bibles, mumbling prayers as they waited to take their turn in the bathroom.

I fell in at the end of the line placing me just outside of Ruth's door. She was leaning against the wooden frame cleaning her glasses with a paper towel and watching the women parade past.

"Store not opening today?" I asked hoping to make small talk and slip back into her good graces. If I'd ever been there.

"Opens at nine."

"You like going there every day?"

She shrugged. "Better than working the farm."

"Must be kind of boring out there in the middle of nowhere. How many customers you get in a day?"

"What are you a census taker? Enough questions. Didn't you learn your lesson yesterday?" She glanced at my foot. "How's it feel?"

I shrugged.

Durable Goods

She put her hand on my shoulder. "Move along."

I stumbled and grabbed a metal footboard to keep from landing on my swollen foot then glanced back at Ruth to see if she'd set me off balance on purpose.

She shook her head and sighed.

On my way to the dining hall I caught up to Sarah who'd fallen far behind the other women. She was pale and held her hand close to her chest.

"How are you?" I asked.

She looked at me and shook her head, her mouth clamped shut.

"You should be in bed," I said. You can't work today."

"I have to," she whispered.

"What are you going to do with one hand?"

"Whatever I can."

"This is fucking ridiculous."

She shot me a glance that told me to drop it.

I picked up a tray and made my way down the line, doubling up on scrambled eggs, sausage and whole-wheat toast, one for me, one for Sarah. At the coffee urn I poured a mug for each of us. She gave me a grateful nod. We settled at a table together though she didn't look up or in any way acknowledge my presence. But when I lifted my toast to take a bite, she threw me an incredulous look.

"Oh yeah," I said dropping the toast back onto my plate. "Give thanks first."

Ruth stood at the front of the room, gave the blessing and a multitude of forks went into motion.

"Where's Isaac?" I asked.

"He often doesn't arrive until after breakfast," Sarah said.

"Late sleeper?"

She didn't respond, but kept her head bowed, eyes on her plate.

"I saw Isaac leave here last night. Does that happen often?"

She glanced at me sideways. "Isaac does what he wants. I don't keep tabs on him."

"But you must hear his truck. Does it go by every night?"

"I hear it sometimes. I have no idea where he's going. Now eat. I don't want to talk."

"How's your hand?"

She ignored me.

After breakfast we gathered our wagons and headed for the trees. I left the laces untied on my right boot, but it wasn't providing much relief. I limped along and made my way toward Sarah who was moving almost as slowly as I was, pulling her wagon with her good hand.

She looked at me surprised. "You don't learn, do you?"

"I'm like a bad penny." I said. That won a smile.

We stopped in front of a couple of Douglas Firs. Hoping like hell I wasn't making a huge mistake, I bent and slipped the picture of Kira out of my sock. I had to trust someone and for now, Sarah was my only option.

I held the photograph in front of her face. "Have you seen her?"

She looked at it closely then turned to me. "Who are you?"

"I'm trying to find my friend. I think she was, or is here. Have you seen her?"

"Are you police?"

"No." I raised my hands in surrender. "I'm just looking for my friend."

"So you're not here because you need to be." She smiled. "That explains a lot."

"I just want to find my friend."

Sarah looked back at the picture and nodded. "She was here. But Isaac took her to the house and I haven't seen her since."

"How long ago did he take her to the house?"

"I don't know."

"How can you not know? She was living here with you."

"We avert our eyes. We keep our mouths shut. It's not spoken of and best forgotten."

"And yet you love him," I shook my head.

"Sometimes he takes a girl right away within a day of her arrival; sometimes, it's months. Some never leave the dorm at all. Time is a hard thing to keep track of here. I think it was the end of last winter when she came. She was with us for maple syrup season and stayed with us all summer. It was sometime in September that he took her, I think. I can't be sure."

"You mean two months ago?"

Sarah nodded. "She was very beautiful. I knew he'd want her as soon as she arrived. I was surprised that he waited as long as he did. But she was difficult. She talked a lot about leaving. She and Ruth argued."

"What did they argue about?"

"She kept saying she wanted to leave, that she was ready to go home. She wanted to see her father. Ruth told her to be quiet, that Isaac would be angry if he heard her. But he must have heard about it because he came for her."

"And you never saw her again?"

She glanced around then dropped to her knees and lifting a small axe, started chopping low branches from the fir tree in front of her with one hand. "I shouldn't say anymore."

"You better watch that ax," I said. "You're not steady."

"Get to work," she whispered.

"Does he have sex with the women in the house?"

"I told you already. I don't know." Her teeth were clenched.

"What is your assumption?"

"It's a husband's right to have sex with his wife." She brushed a tear from her cheek. "You'll find out for yourself. I see it in the way he looks at you. He'll take you next."

I backed away digesting her words. How long did I have before he came for me? Stepping up to a nearby tree I began cutting away misshapen branches leaving only the most pristine, and thought of Isaac weeding out the women. What did he do with the ones he took? I had two days left before Griff and John made their entrance. As much as it scared the hell out of me, I needed Isaac to make his move. When we broke for lunch I'd text Griff with an update and then strap the phone back onto my thigh. I might not have the chance to go back for it later. *'He'll take you next.'* The words sent an icy trail down my back. It's what I wanted. It's why I was here. But I was finding it hard to breathe. I sucked in the scent of pine, hoping it would transport me to images of Christmas instead of the one Sarah had left me with, but sugar plum fairies were few and far between.

A whistle went off in the barn marking the end of work for the morning and commanding us back to the dormitory. After all the women had used the bathroom I went in to take my turn, alone.

My foot throbbed as I stood on the sink and loosened the ceiling grate. Wincing, I lowered myself back onto the tile floor. I needed more of those pills. Sitting on the toilet I texted Griff: *Confirmed Kira was here. Still in the house? Will get inside asap. Xo.* I belted the phone to my thigh the same way Griff had done just before I'd gone into the store to meet Isaac.

I settled on my bunk and flipped open the Bible. The pages fell to Matthew 6:25: *"Don't worry about things---food, drink and clothes."* Wasn't that what Isaac was offering, things? I hadn't seen much spiritual guidance going on anywhere. *"Look at the field lilies!"* Exactly how Isaac wanted the women to see themselves while he treated them like slave labor. They'd simply traded one perpetrator for another the day they'd entered *OK*.

At twelve-thirty Ruth waved her hand over the chimes and we took our places, lining up at the door. As we robotically filed past, she handed each of us a heavy, winter parka, sizes ranged small, medium and large. The women were as excited as kids on Christmas. Now, they could remain in the fields when the temperature dropped to single digits. I slipped mine on and stepped outside reluctantly grateful.

Inside the cafeteria, I placed a square of lasagna on my plate and limped to the table where Sarah sat alone with her head bent. She was an odd duck. Loyal in words, yet she'd deceived him and slept with a migrant.

"What are you going to do now?" she asked when I sat down.

"I need to get into the house and see if my friend is there. I'm not sure how to make that happen."

"It will happen on its own. Be patient."

"I don't have time to be patient."

She looked at me and raised her eyebrows. "You have somewhere to be?"

Afraid I'd said too much, I shook my head. "Just not a patient person."

"This place will teach you."

"Terrific," I said and forked a piece of lasagna into my mouth. After lunch I deposited my plate into the plastic tub by the door and took a breath. I felt anxious as hell. According to the job postings for the afternoon, I was on wreath detail after another half hour of mandatory Bible reading.

Before I reached the door Isaac appeared in front of me blocking my path. I took a step backward, my shoulder blades digging into the plaster wall behind me. Women walked past, their heads bowed. Isaac placed one hand on the wall above my head and leaned into me. He placed one finger close to my nose then ran it whisper soft down over my lips.

"We follow the rules here, one of which is silence when we work and eat. A gaggle of women twittering about nothing of importance is distracting. If you do as I ask you'll reap my reward."

"Your reward or God's?" I tipped my head to the side and offered the hint of a smile hoping to look flirtatious. Not my strong suit, but I needed to stand out one way or another if I was going to get chosen for the house.

Isaac leaned in closer. "I work for Him. You go through me first and I have my own rewards for the women who do what I ask." He dropped his eyes to my breasts, inhaled deeply then looked up and blew his breath softly onto my face, moving my hair just enough to tickle. I squirmed and he smiled. Lowering his hand he slipped it inside my jacket, his knuckles grazing my nipple, his eyes never leaving mine. "It could be nice for you here. I think we'd both be very satisfied." He raised his eyebrows and grinned looking playful and boyish. "Do you understand what I'm saying?"

I smiled back, holding his eyes. "I'll do my best," I whispered.

He stepped back to let me pass. "I'll be watching."

I blinked back tears as I walked toward the dormitory and swallowed hard against the lasagna backpedaling in my throat. I'd sworn to Griff that I could do this. What the hell was I thinking?

When I reached the door of the dormitory, Ruth was waiting. I walked past her but she grabbed me at the elbow stopping me short. She turned my palm over and shoved three white pills into my hand. "How's the foot?"

"These help," I said tossing them into my mouth.

"What did Isaac want?"

"He told me if I play my cards right I'll gain his reward. Lucky me," I said trying to make light of it.

She looked me dead in the eye. "Not everything's a game."

"Are you okay?" Sarah asked as I passed her bed.

I nodded, hesitating beside her. Three things I knew for sure. Isaac Bennett was a lot more than a conduit to God. *Oracles of the Kingdom* was a lot more than a working farm and refuge, and getting out would be a lot harder than getting in.

"What are you two doing?" Ruth stepped up beside us.

"Nothing," Sarah said. "She's not familiar with the Bible. I was just suggesting she read Matthew, Isaac's favorite."

Nice save, I thought and again considered the inconsistencies of the two women. The Eddie Haskells of the group. Meek to Isaac's face, but deviant when it served them, and I was sure that either one of them would let me take the fall if they were caught covering for me. As much as Sarah and I had a connection, her ultimate loyalty was to Isaac. I didn't fault her for it. In this place, you had to protect yourself.

"Well get on your bunks and start reading," Ruth said then disappeared into her room only to reappear ringing those piece of shit chimes a half hour later.

Isaac was astride Job outside the barn when I approached for my afternoon of wreath making. The horse snorted and shook his head pawing the ground as I passed. Before going through the doorway, I glanced back at Isaac. He was staring at me, a smile played at the corner of his mouth. I nodded, acknowledging his attention and stepped inside.

At an open place along the side of the farmer's table I gripped the scarred wood until my legs stopped shaking. A dozen women circled the workspace, their breath sending puffs of smoke into the crisp air. The thought of a Honey Berry cigar made my mouth water. I would kill for one right now. I watched the women's fingers nimbly twisting fir around wire, creating wreaths from a pile of greens in the center of the table. Sarah took the place beside me.

"Did he speak to you?" She asked.

I shook my head and took a deep breath. "Where do you think he was going last night?"

"I told you, I have no idea," she said.

"There were women in the back, the women who live in the house."

She stayed quiet for a long time. I was tying a red velvet ribbon around one of the last wreathes when she stopped working. Her hands lay still on the table. The gauze covering the injured one was brown and sticky with sap.

"Something you want to say?" I asked.

"You don't know that."

"I do in my gut."

She reached over and straightened my bow with her good hand. "What if he did have women in the truck? Where could he possibly be taking them?"

"That's why I need to get into the house. You said he was going to come for me. What's taking so long?"

"He has to be sure."

"Sure of what?"

"That he wants you."

"No test drive?"

She shook her head. "They never come back."

"Why do you think he hasn't taken you?"

"A couple of times I thought he was getting close, but now…" She stopped and looked down at the wreath in her hand.

"The migrant?"

"Now it will never happen."

"So what if he makes a bad choice?"

"If he changes his mind about someone I don't know what happens to them. Like I said, they never come back. "

"I guess I'll find out. Sooner than later he'll realize he made a mistake with me." I stacked my wreath on top of the pile in the center of the table and reached for more pine branches. "When I get into the house, it's not going to be anything good. I think you know that." I looked at Sarah for a response, but she lowered her eyes. "If I find my friend I'm going to take her and get out. And if I find any wrongdoing, I'll expose Isaac. Then you and every woman will be leaving this place. You better start thinking about where you'll go."

"Why are you here? Who are you, really?"

Her questions were so earnest and sincere that I almost told her, but I couldn't risk it. "I told you. I'm here to find a friend."

Isaac had been standing outside of the dining hall when I'd gone in for dinner. His gaze followed me through the cafeteria line, never leaving my face as he offered up thanks for all our blessings. I still wasn't sure if his obvious interest was based in flirtation or intimidation, but whatever the reason, his soulless gaze was unnerving.

In my bunk after lights out, I willed myself to stay awake, listening for the truck. I had to find a way to get close to it, see who was in it, how many, and was one of them Kira? But staying awake was no easy feat after a day spent doing manual labor. I was exhausted. My hands were blistered, my foot purple. Hauling trees and wiring wreathes is not work for wimps.

I waited until shifting bodies had stilled and the light beneath Ruth's door had gone out then I slipped from under my wool blanket and slid down the side of my bed until my socks hit the floor. I slipped my feet into my work boots, laced the left one but kept the right one loose. The tough part would be getting past Ruth's door. She had ears like a German shepherd and the determination to match. But I'd done my homework. I knew it was the third floorboard from the threshold that sounded the alarm. It creaked like a mother…

As I crept past Sarah's bed she raised her head. I placed one finger in front of my lips. She flashed me a fearful look and shook her head. I stepped over the third floorboard and when I reached the door wrapped one hand around the chimes. With the other, I lifted them from their nail and kneeling, laid them onto the wooden floor. The deadbolt slid back smoothly and as slowly as my rush of adrenaline would allow, I turned the knob.

A waft of cold air hit me in the face as I stepped into the darkness. After securing the door, I hesitated waiting to hear Ruth's angry bark, but the only sound was an owl perched in the branches overhead. I walked down the dirt road staying close to the tree line and the shadows it provided. When I was close to the main road I crouched in a clump of bushes off to the side. From there I would be able to see the truck coming and do a head count when it slowed in front of me before easing out onto the main road.

At least an hour had passed. My feet and hands were numb and I was just beginning to think this had been a stupid idea when I saw headlights bouncing toward me. My heart picked up speed and I crouched lower, burying myself among the bushes so the beams wouldn't give me away. The truck rolled closer and so did my opportunity to get a look inside the bed. The taillights brightened as the driver braked at the edge of the road before pulling out. Hats and winter coats made it hard to see any details, but these were no migrant men. They were too small. Five women huddled together, their arms around one another for support or warmth or both. I couldn't make out faces just hair straggling out from beneath wool hats, blond, brown, mostly nondescript in the darkness.

As they pulled onto the main road one of the figures stiffened, her head turned toward me. She was wearing a white ski parka. Dark hair tumbled over its fur collar and fell almost to her waist. I couldn't see her eyes, but I knew she was looking right at me. Her body language said she'd seen me. We watched each other until the distance between us rendered us both out of sight. I turned and started back toward the dormitory hoping to slip in as easily as I'd slipped out.

There was no light beneath the door as I approached and I took that as a sign that Ruth was still in her room sleeping unaware. Opening the door with one slow, continuous turn of the knob, I stepped inside and closed it soundlessly behind me.

A hand wrapped around my neck pinning me tight against the door.

"Where the fuck were you?"

"I, I…outside. I needed air."

"There's air in here."

"Move your hand, Ruth. I can't breathe."

She dropped her hand and stared at me, waiting.

"I just went outside for a minute. I was sweating."

"Sweating? It's November not July. What do you mean you were sweating?"

"I don't know. I didn't feel good. I wanted cold air."

"You're a liar. Why are these on the floor?" She kicked the chimes with the toe of her slipper. They sang across the floorboards.

I just wanted some fresh air and I didn't want to wake everybody so I took them down. Where the hell do you think I'm gonna go? We're in the middle of nowhere."

"Do you know what he'll do to you if he finds you out walking around at night?"

"Stick my hand in the fire?"

"Don't be a wise-ass. You better hope you never find out. Now get the fuck in your bed."

"Does that mean you're not going to tell on me?"

"I told you before you're mouth's gonna get you in trouble. Stop asking questions."

She shoved me away from the door and into the aisle.

I landed on my bad foot. My leg buckled and I hit the floor. A few heads rose from their pillows.

"Go to sleep," Ruth said. "All of you." She picked up the chimes and returned them to the nail above the door then walked to her bedroom without giving me a second glance.

I wrapped the wool blanket around me and snuggled into my bunk. I was freezing and thanks to Ruth, my foot was throbbing. At least I'd confirmed my suspicion that Isaac was transporting the girls. Where to was my next question? I didn't think Ruth would tell him about my little escapade. It would reflect on her as much as on me and I was beginning to wonder if Ruth was really the good little soldier Isaac thought she was.

GRIFF

John was standing behind his desk when Griff half-knocked his way into the room.

"Kira was there," he said.

John let go of the paper he was holding, letting it float feather-like to the worn, wooden desktop. His eyes stayed on Griff. "Was?"

"Britt said she was there, but doesn't know if she still is. From what she's said so far, which isn't much, it sounds like most women work on the farm, but some get taken into his house. She's trying to find a way to get inside."

"She safe?"

"Doesn't sound safe to me, but she won't say that, wants to be a hero. She's got something to prove."

"To you?"

Griff shook his head. "To herself, to her mother, to her sister…old wounds run deep."

"That's what this is about?" John sat in his desk chair and ran a hand over his grey, military cut. "Redemption?"

"She wants to help you, but I know there's more to it than being a Samaritan. It's a two birds with one stone kind of thing. The more I think about it, the less I like it. I'm this close to going in after her."

"You gave her four days." John said. He walked to the window and looked out onto a muddy parking lot bordered with black crusty snow that the plow had left behind.

"I know what I said, but I might have been wrong."

"Stop second guessing yourself. This is the first time I've gotten close. We can't pull Britt out yet. Especially now that she knows Kira was there."

"So we risk the safety of one for the safety of the other?"

The two men stared at each other without speaking.

Griff broke away first. "I want to find Kira too, but not at Britt's expense."

"Britt's a capable PI. She'll get out if she needs to."

"She's young and insecure and she thinks finding Kira will change all that."

"Won't it?"

"Jesus, John."

"What if it was Allie? Would you send her in then?"

"That's not fair."

"Why? C'mon Griff. This is what we do. This is the nature of the game and Britt isn't stupid. She knew what she was getting into."

"I don't think she did. I'm willing to bet she's in over her head."

"Then she'll get out."

"Not if she drowns first," Griff said walking out and slamming the door behind him.

OK
WEDNESDAY

We'd been cutting trees all morning and when the lunchtime whistle went off I was more than ready for a break. I'm not a wimp, but I like to get my exercise inside a heated gym or better yet, under Griff's blankets. I'd barely slept last night thinking about the truck and the women in it.

Ruth was standing outside the dormitory as I approached. I hesitated, giving her a questioning look, asking if she'd told Isaac about last night.

He'd been in the field watching us cut all morning. Each time I wrestled a fir onto the flatbed he'd let out a little *"mmm, mmm"* of approval. I'd waited for my punishment to come assuming Ruth had told him, but his expression was one of seduction not anger whenever I'd stolen a glance.

Ruth looked at me now and shook her head once. "No," she said. "I didn't."

I walked down the aisle of the dormitory and lay on my bunk, relieved that she hadn't told, scared of what was coming and angry at feeling so powerless. This place was right out of Twilight Zone, all around me passive submission to a lunatic, me included. The anticipation was making me as crazy as the others. *Come and get me, Isaac, I whispered. I'm ready for you.* Looking back now, I'd say be careful what you wish for.

Exhausted from my lack of sleep last night or from my building unease, I closed my eyes. Within seconds I was in my office, Griff perched on the corner of my desk. I was just starting to tell him about the dream I'd been having when

Ruth clanged her chimes and jolted me back to reality. It was time for lunch. Twenty-eight pairs of feet hit the floor.

I stepped inside the cafeteria and slid my tray down the line of offerings. My anxiety made it hard to focus, and the decision between hot dogs or grilled cheese became a real dilemma.

"Move it along."

I turned to the voice and found Isaac standing behind me, too close. His breath brushed my neck, making me shiver. It was coming. I could feel it.

I stepped past him and crossed the room setting my tray down on one of the long cafeteria tables and taking a seat across from Sarah. "Truce?" I asked and held up my right hand as if swearing to the promise. "No more shop talk."

She smiled. "Thank you."

"What's on the agenda for the afternoon?"

"Wreaths."

"Huh?"

"Wreaths."

"Wreaths?"

"You asked what we're doing this afternoon."

"Oh, yeah," I said looking back at Isaac, his black eyes bearing down. "Right." I turned to Sarah and took a breath. "I'm not very good at making wreaths. I think I got shortchanged on the gene for creativity."

She laughed.

My sandwich was stuck in my throat as I took my place among the eight women in various stages of assembling wreaths. The others were in the field cutting and gathering trees.

I'd been here two full days and it was already early afternoon of the third. I only knew that Kira had been here, not whether she still was. If I made it into the house and she wasn't there, I had a little over twenty-four hours to find out where she'd gone before Griff came in.

There was a rustling at the door and Isaac stepped into the barn, his eyes never left mine as he made his approach. At the table, he took the branches from my hands and gave them to Sarah. "I want you to come with me." Without waiting for an answer, he wrapped his fingers around my arm and steered me away from the rest of them.

At the door I pulled out of his grip and turned back to Sarah. "Don't forget what I told you."

She looked quickly away and began arranging the boughs, unwilling to implicate herself.

"Where are you taking me?" I asked.

He kept my elbow firmly in his grasp as we moved toward his truck.

"I thought you might like to see my house. You asked about it when you first arrived. We're preparing for a little holiday party. I want you to be a part of it."

No doubt it would be a party I'd never forget. "'What about my things at the dormitory? I should get them."

He looked at me the same way he had that day at the market, with an air of confidence emanating power and control. "Everything you need is in my house."

Not quite, I thought and felt for my cell phone. If he found it, it would be the end of our operation and probably me too, but if I failed to contact Griff, he and John would be breaking down Isaac's door. Keeping it on me was my only option at the moment.

Isaac reached over and took my hand stroking my fingers with his thumb. It was all I could do not to jerk my hand away. A smile played on his lips as we bounced over ruts. I stuffed my other hand beneath my thigh and kept my eyes on the house as we approached. In its younger days it had probably been a stately family dwelling and a beauty at that. I could imagine a gathering of rocking chairs on the wide farmer's porch. Knitting and babies in the laps of women sharing ice tea and gossip.

We came to a stop and climbed the front steps, now nothing more than warped wooden slats. Scattered pieces of hay and straw slid over the dusty pine boards, forming random shadows against the faded, yellow paint. At the far end of the porch, a pitchfork leaned against the clapboards, done for the day.

At the top of the stairs Isaac pulled a set of keys from his pocket. He freed three deadbolts, each with a different key. The locks were overkill. I could have splintered the weathered wood with one swift kick. The door groaned open and I stepped inside.

A veil of smoke drifted from a room to my right hovering overhead in the hallway. Isaac nodded me across the wide pine floorboards toward the French doors. A threadbare Oriental carpet covered the floor. Victorian couches and chairs hugged graying walls that had once been white. Above the furniture religious pictures hung in ornate, gold frames, Christ with a crown of thorns plunged into His head, The Last Supper, The Road to Damascus.

Beneath the pictures, sprawled on the couches were women in lacy bras and underwear, their hair unkempt, their feet bare. Some wore sheer blouses over their bras, or bathrobes hanging open. Each held a cigarette in one hand. When I entered the room eight pairs of vacant eyes looked up.

Isaac hovered behind me, too close. His breath warmed my neck. He placed one hand on each of my shoulders and then let them fall to my breasts, giving them a gentle squeeze.

I pulled away and spun around, knocking his hands aside with my forearm.

He laughed and let go. "Welcome to my family," he said. Looking past me, his eyes roamed the women finally settling on a young girl in a baby doll ensemble of purple paisley.

"Elizabeth, take Mary upstairs. Show her to her room and help her change her clothes."

"My name is Britt," I said.

"Not anymore. Now it's Mary, as in Magdalene," he laughed.

Elizabeth stood and crossed the room without a word. Her hand grazed my elbow as she passed.

"Go," Isaac said nodding toward her.

I followed the girl up the carpeted staircase and down a hallway with bedrooms on either side. There was something familiar about her that I couldn't place. At the end of the hall she stepped into the room on her left.

"Where's the bathroom?" I asked. If I was going to be dressing like the women downstairs there'd be no where to attach my cell phone on my body where it wouldn't be seen. I needed to ditch it before anyone realized I had it.

"You have to change first." She pointed to the bed in the far corner of the room. "That's yours. Your clothes are on top."

An ivory, satin negligee lay across the bed.

"Looks like I'm getting married."

"The first night you're here you spend with Isaac. He likes to think of it as the beginning of your relationship. Like a wedding night."

I looked at her, horrified. "I'm not sleeping with him."

"He doesn't ask often." Her voice was low and seductive. "It's usually just the first night, unless you make an impression." She gave a throaty laugh.

"There's not going to be a first night," I said trying to hold my voice steady. "And you better believe I'll make an impression." I turned and looked at her again. "Where's the bathroom?"

"Give me your clothes." She nodded to the blue sweatshirt with *OK* on the front and my jeans. "You don't need those anymore." She stretched one arm toward me for the clothes I had yet to take off. "It's not so bad here. We get what we need."

"Your needs and mine don't fall into the same category."

"Not yet," she said.

I ignored her prophecy and pointed to her scantily clad body. "I'm not dressing like that every day."

"Isaac likes us like this. Anyway, who cares? When we go out he gives us other things to wear, dresses and sweaters and coats."

I thought of the truck pulling out of the driveway. Hopefully I could find one woman who would be willing to talk. From the slow lilt of Elizabeth's voice whatever was in her system kept everything right with the world. There'd been a strong smell of pot downstairs mingled with tobacco.

"I'm not changing until I go to the bathroom," I said again.

She lay her head back onto the bed and slid her legs straight. "Suit yourself, but hurry up. It's over there." She pointed to a closed door in the corner of the room.

"Does every room have its own bathroom?"

She nodded.

"How many girls live here?"

"There're five bedrooms, two or three beds in each. Sometimes they're full, sometimes not."

"Where are the rest of the girls?"

"How should I know? It's a big house."

"Doesn't Isaac keep tabs on them? What if they try to leave?"

She rolled huge brown eyes toward me. "Why would they?"

I grabbed the nightgown off the bed and stepped into the bathroom. There was no lock on the door. I slipped my jeans down and unstrapped the phone from my thigh. My hands were shaking. What was I going to tell Griff? That Isaac and I were about to share our wedding night? He'd freak and ruin the whole thing. I had to at least get the information I'd come for. I held the phone between shaking hands and texted Griff. *Inside the house. Prostitution? No sign of Kira yet. More tomorrow.* I hit SEND then powered it down.

There was a narrow door to my right and I lifted the latch. Inside, shelves were lined with towels, shampoo bottles and boxes of tampons. With one foot on the toilet, I was able to see onto the top shelf. A roll of wallpaper, dusty with age, lay against the far wall, a box of mothballs in front of it, nothing that anyone would be reaching for anytime soon. I set the phone and Kira's picture on the shelf and slid it back as far as I could then I hopped off the toilet and replaced the latch.

"Hurry up." Elizabeth's drawl came from the other side of the door. "Isaac's calling for us."

I pulled the negligee over my head and caught sight of myself in the mirror. It was too long and made for D-cups. I wasn't even close. Swallowing back humiliation, I reminded myself that no one I knew was going to see me, and Griff would never have to know.

"Okay, I'm ready," I said tossing my clothes to Elizabeth.

She laughed. "Your black bikinis are showing."

"Can't help it."

"He wants you in nothing but what he gives you. That means the nightgown only."

I hesitated, my heart doing back flips, afraid of exposure in every sense of the word. Then I tossed her my underwear too.

"You're a good girl. He's going to like you," she said and giggled.

I followed Elizabeth downstairs and back into the room we'd come from. I'd be hard pressed to give it a name. The Victorian style furniture, draped with half-dressed women suggested a whorehouse straight out of an old, western movie, but the religious décor brought me right back to the convent at my Catholic elementary school. If nothing else, Isaac was eclectic. It was mid-afternoon. Each of the women in the room, which now had grown to eleven including Elizabeth and me, had a cocktail at hand.

A deep chuckle behind me brought goose bumps to my flesh. I turned to see Isaac eyeing me up and down. "Guess I don't have your size," he said. Curling his index finger over the top of the nightgown, he pulled it out and away from my body then stepped forward and dropped his eyes inside the silky material inspecting me from neck to feet. He nodded approvingly and nuzzled his cheek against mine. "The good Lord sure knows what He's doing," he whispered in my ear. "I'll find your size. Work like that deserves to be shown off in a flattering light."

Isaac crossed the room toward the alcove that housed the bar. It was no larger than a walk-in closet, but it didn't need to be. It was stocked well enough to satisfy even the thirstiest woman in the house.

"Wine or mixed?" he asked me over his shoulder.

I shook my head. "Neither."

"Neither is not an option," he said. His voice had switched from seductive to commanding in the seconds it took him to walk across the room. He looked at me. His eyes turned cold and dark.

"Wine," I said. "Red."

His smile returned. "Lovely choice. May I suggest a Cabernet?"

I nodded. My legs wobbled. For the first time I was glad for my oversized nightgown. I'd done exactly what I'd told Griff and John I could do. I was inside. I should be feeling a little smug and pleased with myself, but all I felt was fear. What the hell had I gotten into? Standing in that room, watching him come toward me drink in hand, I knew one thing for certain. I wasn't nearly as brave as I pretended to be. I wanted to find Kira and give Griff reason to believe in me, to recognize my worth and change the goddamn sign from Cole & Co. to Cole and Callahan. But right now? I was having second thoughts on all counts.

He handed me a goblet and watched until I'd taken a sip then he smiled and turned toward the others, all of who had been watching me as though it were some rite of passage.

Isaac touched my cheek with his fingertips and smirked. "I have things to attend to, my little Mary Magdalene. While I'm working, you get the feel of your new home and meet your sisters," he said. "And then, tonight will be ours."

I assumed I was supposed to look pleased, but a wave of nausea hit me and my scalp tingled with sweat. I drew a breath and forced a smile, but he'd already turned away from me. Just before passing through the doorway he slapped the young girl nearest him on the back of her head. "Go easy on the booze," he said. "You're working tonight."

Her mouth hit the rim of her glass and it fell to the floor.

"And for Christ's sake, clean that up."

She walked to the bar like a foal on new legs, retrieved a dishrag and collapsed back over the spill. She dabbed at the puddle of vodka then sat back on her heels, swayed and took a gulp from the bottle in her hand.

Elizabeth knelt beside her. "I've got it," she said. "Go pass out somewhere else."

And then it dawned on me where I'd seen Elizabeth before. She was the one with the long dark hair I'd seen in the truck. She must have felt my eyes on her because she looked up and met my gaze. "What the hell are you lookin' at?"

"I shook my head. "Nothing."

"Well go do nothing somewhere else." She went back to blotting the vodka from the rug. A couple of the women behind me laughed.

I sank into an unoccupied chair and sipped my wine. Alcohol was the last thing I wanted right now, but I had to play the part. Thankfully I didn't know at this moment how far the role would take me.

Across the room, the girl who'd dropped her drink wedged herself into the corner of a maroon, velvet couch.

She lifted a pipe to her lips, lit it and took a long draw, closing her eyes and tilting her head back. The smell of marijuana filled the room. Before she could get the pipe back to her mouth it slipped from her hand, hit her thigh and landed on the cushion beside her. Its contents spilled onto the velvet.

"Jesus Christ." The woman beside her jumped from the couch and grabbed the pipe. She brushed the glowing ashes onto the floor and stepped them. "What the fuck? Watch what you're doing."

But the girl was out cold. A thin strand of drool connecting chin to chest. The woman tossed the pipe onto the coffee table and wandered to the bar shaking her head. No one else in the room showed any reaction. The afternoon passed with their lifeless eyes staring at the Oriental rug or searching the distance outside the window. I sat among them sipping wine wondering what went on inside their heads, if anything. No one seemed interested in leaving or even capable. What did that say about Kira and my plan to rescue her? I emptied my glass of Cabernet and left it on the bar. Hearing dishes rattling down the hallway, I followed the sound into the kitchen.

"Hurry up, Rose." Isaac was seated at the table. A woman stood at the stove holding a wooden spoon making figure eights in a cast iron pot. A young girl was setting the farmhouse table with plates and silverware. He looked up as I walked into the room. "Go get the others, Mary," he said. "Dinner."

I retraced my steps and leaned into the living room. "Time to eat," I said. A couple of the women stood and came toward me, the rest went to the bar for refills. The girl passed out on the couch didn't move.

I took a seat at the opposite end of the table as far from Isaac as possible. Rose dished spoonfuls of Mac and cheese onto the plates. Chair legs dragged over the wooden floor as each of the women took a place. Rose sat in the chair beside Isaac. She was older than the rest of us and I wondered about her role in the house. She wasn't turning any tricks at her age. The meal was dead silent except for the occasional burp, drunken slurping and tobacco-laden coughs. I'd barely inhaled the last spoonful when the young girl who'd set the table stood to clear the plates.

"You, you, you and you," Isaac said pointing to four of the women. "Make yourselves presentable. We have an engagement. Where's our fifth?"

"Out cold." Elizabeth smiled at Isaac.

"Christ," he said. "I'm too good to you girls."

"That's what I tell them," Rose said.

"Shut up, Rose." Isaac turned to me. "Very soon you'll be working too. The better your performance the more often you go out. It's all about creating a demand. We'll discuss that later." He smiled.

My stomach turned. I dropped my eyes to my plate hoping my mac and cheese wasn't going to rebel.

The young girl who'd been clearing our dishes moved from the sink back to the table and stacked two plates on her forearm, waitress style, then reached for Isaac's but stumbled. The stacked dishes slipped from her arm onto his thigh leaving remnants of uneaten pasta and cheese on his jeans. Rose and the others froze, not a breath broke the silence.

"Stupid," he yelled, rising to his feet.

The plates crashed to the floor. He stood a foot from the young girl and swung back his arm, tossing steaming coffee from his cup onto her chest. She screamed as the scalding liquid hit her turning the white lace of her negligee a dirty brown and the skin beneath it, pink as a newborn pig.

Isaac dropped his empty mug to the floor with the broken plates. "Clean this up," he said to her. "You're my number five tonight. Let's see if you can get this right."

At the doorway he hesitated and turned back to me. "Can you see now Mary, why I needed a new girl in the house?

Rose ran cold water on a cloth and held it against the young girl's chest while two others cleaned the floor. No one noticed me watching until they were done. And then Rose looked at me. "Don't make mistakes," she said.

The girl stood beside Rose, whimpering. "Where's he taking me?"

Rose shook her head. "You'll see. You'll be fine. Go get dressed, hurry. The girl left the kitchen and I heard her feet pounding up the stairs. I remembered Ruth's words. *Isaac doesn't like it if you're late.*

A few minutes later the four women he'd pointed out during dinner and the now defunct house girl came down the stairs dressed in outdoor clothing and winter jackets. I saw the white parka on Elizabeth. Rose took the elbow of the girl who'd dropped the plates and walked with her onto the porch. She was crying.

"Just do whatever they tell you," Rose said.

The young girl nodded, wiping her nose on the sleeve of her jacket and climbed into the back of the truck with the others.

I stood in the doorway, watching until Rose came back inside, closed the front door and slid the deadbolts into place. She glanced into the living room where the others had resumed their drinking and getting high. "Finish cleaning the kitchen," she said to me and retreated upstairs.

I went back to the kitchen glad to have something to do that would provide at least a bit of normalcy. If washing dishes was my only option I'd take it. I ran the plates under hot water reviewing each of the girls in my head. I needed someone I could talk to. Someone who could shed light on what the hell was going on here.

Durable Goods

The back door swung open startling me and Ruth came into the kitchen carrying a brown paper bag in each arm. "So you're the new house girl?" She laughed.

"Right now, I have no idea what I am. New girl in the house or new house girl, what's the difference?"

She set the bags on the kitchen table and laughed. "A house girl is the maid. A girl in the house makes money. I knew that other one wouldn't last. She was too stupid for Isaac's taste." Ruth carried containers of milk and orange juice and a package of butter to the refrigerator. "Got any coffee?"

My hands shook as I held a mug in one and poured from the carafe with the other. "Don't spill, don't spill, " I repeated in my head and then handed Ruth the full cup.

She looked at me as she took it. "Thanks," she said.

There was something in her voice, something like sincerity or empathy and I wondered if I'd heard right. Or was I so desperate that I'd imagined it?

She sat at the table and I began unpacking what was left in the bags.

"I'll do it," she said.

And there it was again…kindness. I'd heard right.

"It's okay," I said. "I have to figure out where things go if I'm going to be the house girl." Our eyes met and held, but neither of us mentioned my misconstrued words. I put away Frosted Flakes and Captain Crunch, Oreos, Ice Cream, canned vegetables and twelve cans of Campbell's soup and wondered where all the farm vegetables and meat went. From the looks of what the cupboards held, not to us.

When I finished I poured myself a cup of coffee and sat across from Ruth, not sure if it was okay for me to sit, but she didn't say anything and I could feign ignorance until I learned the ropes. It occurred to me that being young, Kira might have started out as a house girl. Maybe she and Ruth had become friends and Ruth had mailed the postcard. I could show Ruth the picture. It would be a huge risk, but I had to start taking a few if I was going to get anywhere.

"So, if I'm the house girl, what am I supposed to do?"

"I don't think that's Isaac's plan for you," Ruth said.

"Once he sees how well I perform in this role, he won't need to check my performance in the other."

Ruth pursed her lips and shook her head, but let my fantasy slide. "Everything from laundry to vacuuming to preparing meals. I told him he needs more than one person, but that would cut into profits." She rinsed her cup at the sink and put it back on the shelf. "C'mon, I'll show you where the laundry is."

I followed her down a rickety set of worn wooden stairs into a dark, dingy rat hole farmhouse basement. A washer and dryer sat up on cement blocks in one corner, a plastic laundry basket in front of them.

"You have to go room to room looking for dirty stuff. They aren't very good at remembering to use a hamper, too fucked up," she added.

We headed back up the stairs.

"I bring the groceries so if there's something you want, you have to let me know."

"What about some protein, meat, fish, eggs?"

She shrugged, "That's doubtful. Isaac prefers carbs. They're filling and cheap."

"And protein is brain food. We might actually be able to think," I added.

She looked at me for a minute like a parent surprised by a child's knowledge. "Whatever," she said and crossed the kitchen. At the door she hesitated, turning back. "All that stuff will be coming, but it's for the party."

"Party?"

"Isaac's holiday gathering."

"When's that?"

"Friday night. He has it every year. And just so you know. House girl or not, you'll be a girl of the house that night."

I leaned back against the counter, gripped it with both hands and watched Ruth leave. *Don't freak out. That's forty-eight hours away. A lot can happen between now and then.*

With no clocks in the house it was impossible to keep track of time. The girls and Isaac hadn't returned. I'd downed a third glass of wine hoping it would lessen my anxiety over what would happen when he did. I could go to bed, but there was no way I'd close my eyes knowing he was coming back for me. Looking around the living room, it was obvious that I was the only coherent woman in the house, except for Rose, but she'd disappeared upstairs. Maybe she'd gone to bed. It seemed like a good time to slip away and text Griff.

I watched for a follower as I crept up the stairs and into the bedroom, but no one seemed aware of my absence. Closing the bedroom door as quietly as I could, I went into the bathroom and took my cell from its hiding place in the closet. Griff had texted.

I don't like you being in the house. Not safe. Stebbins says we're wrong about Bennett. If I don't hear from you tonight I'm coming tomorrow.

I relaxed a little. He had my back.

No Kira, but give me more time. Party Friday. Will send details. Wait to hear from me.

Against everything my head told me, I'd just asked for more time. But even if we didn't find Kira, we could bust open Isaac's little prostitution ring. And who knew where that might lead. I put the phone back in the closet and opened the bathroom door. There was a figure sitting on my bed across the room, even in the darkness I knew it was Isaac. I froze.

"You're not supposed to be up here alone. Until you understand how things work someone needs to accompany you."

"When did you get back?" I asked, hoping to shift the focus away from my disobedience.

"Where's Rose? She should have been keeping an eye on you."

"I, I don't know. I think she went to bed. I had to pee. Someone was in the bathroom downstairs and everyone else was, well…not worth asking."

He smiled, getting the joke. Lifting a goblet of wine, he motioned with his other hand for me to come to him. I met his eyes, took the glass and sipped from it. It was a different brand, too tangy.

"I like the other one better."

"This one's more expensive. Drink it."

"Money doesn't make it taste better."

"Drink it down," he said. He stood and waited until I'd swallowed most of the wine. When I had, he took me by the hand and led me from the room and down the stairway.

At the foot of the steps, I tripped. He laughed and pulled me along. I reached for the wall to steady myself but it slipped away from my hand and I couldn't find it again. The realization that he'd drugged me began to take hold, but floated away before I could get a firm grasp.

I looked around to see where he was taking me. We entered the kitchen. Pans waved overhead from the ceiling rack and floated past us. I banged into the refrigerator and smacked my shoulder on the handle. "That'll leave a bruise," I heard a voice say, but wasn't sure if it had been mine, or Isaac's.

He pulled me into an alcove behind the mop closet and up a tiny, winding staircase that moments ago had been completely hidden from view, at least from my view, but in my present condition that wasn't saying much. At the top of the stairs another hallway lay ahead of us. There were rooms on either side, though all were dark and empty, maybe maid's quarters, once upon a time. I laughed out loud at the words once upon a time, like I was telling a bedtime story.

What a fucking bedtime story, I thought and laughed again. I knew there was nothing funny about what was happening, but it all seemed so ridiculous. We entered the room on the right. Isaac let go of my hand, leaned behind me and closed the door.

A canopy bed hovered two feet off the ground. White satin sheets and pillows floated above it. He flipped a wall switch beside the door and a dim light spread over the room. Turning to face me, he lifted the straps of my nightgown off my shoulders. It landed in a pile around my feet.

"What the hell…" I bent and reached for the gown too quick. A wave of nausea hit me, I swayed, dizzy and my knees hit the floor.

Isaac laughed and knelt in front of me. Cupping my breasts in his palms.

I waved my forearm and broke his hold, but the movement toppled me over.

He grabbed my shoulder and flipped me onto my back. With one knee on my chest holding me in place he studied the scars on my stomach, tracing them with his fingertip. "Will make-up cover these?" he asked.

"Get off me," I said landing my fist against his chest, but my arms were like rubber. There was no force behind the blow.

"Answer me." He dug his knee into my chest.

"They're from a long time ago. I wasn't a happy kid."

"I don't give a shit what they're from. I want them covered up."

Whatever he'd put in my wine was beginning to release its hold. Maybe he'd only used enough to get me upstairs and into this room and as my head cleared fear took hold. "Get off me you sick fuck," I said. I swung my fist at his chest again, but it was like moving under water.

Isaac laughed and his eyes lit up. I'd been right. He liked a fight. I squirmed beneath his knee trying to wriggle free. He grabbed both of my wrists in one hand and wrapped his other arm around my waist. Lifting me from the floor, he carried me to the bed and dropped me onto satin sheets then took a step back, surveying.

I sat up, my head spinning and tried to scoot off the bed. The hammering in my ears was so loud I couldn't hear. He shoved me back with one hand on my forehead. I sat again, and again he shoved me back, this time with his boot on my chest. I looked up at him. He stood over me, waiting. That's when I knew that I wasn't getting out of this.

I wanted more of whatever had been in my wine, anything that would deaden me to what was coming. I thought of Griff and felt humiliated and ashamed, apologizing to him over and over in my head for being so stupid. "I want more of that wine," I said.

"He shook his head. "You're gonna remember this." With a palm on either side of my head, he straddled me and lowered his mouth to mine.

I twisted to the side. He grabbed my shoulder and shoved me back, his mouth on my neck. I landed my fist on the side of his head.

He laughed and sat up. "I love a good fight," he said. "Makes it much more exciting."

Sitting back on his heels he took off his belt and bound my wrists above my head. He started to push my legs apart. I squeezed my thighs together like I was barrel racing a quarter horse and squirmed side to side. He landed a fist on my right thigh. A Charlie-horse made me cry out and ended my struggling. Pushing my legs open, he knelt between them. I heard the zipper on his pants. My eyes found the ceramic light fixture on the ceiling over the bed. Through a blur of tears I traced roses and leaves and tried to be anywhere but where I was. Then the pounding started. First it was feet on the stairs then down the hallway then a fist on the bedroom door.

"Isaac, Isaac," a voice called.

"I'm busy."

"Lucas is here. He wants to see you now."

"Jesus Christ," he said. "Tell him to wait."

"He won't. He wants you now."

"Fucking prima-donna," Isaac said standing and pulling up his pants. He reached for my arms and tore the belt from my wrists.

I winced, but he didn't notice.

He opened the door, stepped into the hall and slammed it behind him.

I pushed off the bed. My feet hit the floor and I swayed like a toddler; whatever had been in that wine was not completely gone. I gripped the bed for stability and inched toward my nightgown. There was shouting coming from below me. Around me everything in the room floated like gravity had deserted. I crawled to the door and opened it, gripped the doorframe and pulled myself upright. Looking down the hallway, I realized now that these rooms must have once been the staff's quarters. Hugging the wall I made it down the narrow staircase that led to the kitchen. Fluorescent lights brought tears to my eyes. People brushed past me, but took no notice.

When I reached the parlor door I took a right and started up the main stairway crawling on all fours for balance. I was elated when I reached the bedroom and found it empty. I collapsed onto my bed. From the yelling and crying below me, it sounded as though everyone was still downstairs. Lying still, the fog inside my head began to clear. A prone position was definitely preferable to vertical, maybe that was the point. Griff was out there somewhere staring at his phone waiting to hear from me. But I didn't think I could make it to the bathroom, let alone send a coherent text. And even if I did, what would I tell him? I closed my eyes and the chaos below me slipped away.

Moonlight reflected off unfamiliar yellow walls. I looked for the row of dormitory bunks, but saw only two other beds in the room. Slowly, it came to me that I was in my bedroom inside Isaac's house. Filmy, nicotine stained curtains waved in a frigid breeze coming from the partially opened window. I rose to close it and squinted at my reflection in the darkened windowpane, feeling like someone had slammed me in the head with a two-by-four. A vague memory of lying beneath Isaac came to mind.

"Shut the fucking window," a voice said from the other side of the room. I turned to see Elizabeth coming out of the bathroom.

"Working on it," I said. I started to push against the paint chipped frame, but stopped at the sound of a car engine. Outside, Isaac was standing beside the driver's door of a police car that said St. Bart Sheriff on the side. I let out a sigh of relief; they were here for me. Griff had sent them ahead and any minute he and John would come careening down the long, dirt driveway in CID's black Suburban. But then I heard Isaac laugh and a second later an arm came out of the cruiser's window and he and the driver shook hands. Sheriff Stebbins and Isaac? It would explain why Stebbins hadn't had time for us the day we'd driven up to talk to him. We'd had no reason to suspect him as being anything but truthful, albeit not much help. Now here he was sitting in the driveway, him and Isaac shaking hands. I heard footsteps behind me and turned to see Rose standing in the middle of the room.

"What are you looking at?" she asked.

"I thought I heard something outside, but it's nothing." I lowered the window.

She came up beside me and looked out. The cruiser had disappeared. She nodded. "Get some sleep. You'll be making breakfast soon."

I sat up straight. The cold air and the sight of Isaac and Stebbins had rendered me fully awake. "Are you in charge?"

She looked like she didn't know how to interpret my question.

"I'm just asking 'cause I don't know who to go to if I have questions. I mean Ruth showed me the laundry but she's not always here."

"Ruth." Rose said the name like it was the punch line of a joke and laughed. "Ruth has nothing to do with this house. She runs errands that's all."

I thought again of Kira's postcard. Had Ruth run that errand? "Isn't she Isaac's daughter?"

"So what?"

"Why doesn't she live in the house?"

Rose laughed again and ran a hand through her wild, red hair. "Have you looked at her? Isaac has his pride."

"But she's his daughter."

"A point you shouldn't make to him, if you're smart. Anyway, Ruth's happier in combat boots than negligees so it works for everyone. And yeah, I'm in charge in the house, sort of. Clients tend to like 'em young, but I make sure I'm useful to Isaac in other ways, like keepin' you girls in line. Enough chitchat. It's almost time to get up," she said and disappeared from the door.

Elizabeth had slipped into the bed across from mine and now rolled toward me. "What the fuck, are you doing in here?"

"Nice mouth," I answered knowing I shouldn't throw stones.

"I thought you were with Isaac."

"Whatever happened with someone named Lucas canceled that out. I guess you could say he saved me." I said it without thinking, but regretted my words immediately. I was supposed to be grateful that Isaac had brought me to the house.

"He was here for a girl. Too bad nobody saved her." Elizabeth's voice was monotone.

"What do you mean?"

"The girl that dropped her drink and passed out on the couch. She was supposed to work last night. But she's always too drunk. Isaac reached his limit with her so he shipped her out. Lucas came to pick her up."

"Who's Lucas?"

"A buyer."

"A buyer?"

"Jesus, what do you live under a rock?" She leaned up on one elbow and looked at me. Her black hair was a mass of tangles, but her face was beautiful. Hazel eyes and full lips dominated a Mediterranean complexion. "You really are new," she said.

"So Isaac sold her to Lucas?"

"That's how it goes. When Isaac gets tired of us Lucas finds us a new home. She was a pain in the ass. Clients don't want a puking whore. If you work hard Isaac keeps you."

"Tell me about the work."

"You'll find out for yourself."

"I don't want to."

She laughed. "Then what the fuck are you doing here? It's what we do. Anyway, it's not like you have a choice. You're working for him now."

"I worked for him out on the farm."

"Not that kind of work," she said. "That's not what you do in the house."

"Then tell me."

"You bring in the money that keeps the farm running and you keep his clients satisfied."

"The women in the dormitory say he saved them. Did he save you too?"

"If you call screwing some cigar-smoking, fat-assed old fart being saved then, yeah, call me saved."

She stood and the blanket slipped to the floor. Naked, she crossed the room and picked up a pack of cigarettes from the dresser. Her young body was as beautiful as her face. Long and lean, but ample where it mattered. When she turned her back to me, it was covered with pencil thin red lines. Old scars.

"Make-up covers them," she said when she noticed me staring. She sat back on her bed and pulled the blanket around her.

I remembered Isaac saying the same thing to me when he saw the scars on my stomach. But mine were not from some deranged customer's whip; they were from my own pre-teen hand, my own warped way of overriding the feelings of worthlessness that dovetailed my mother's indifference.

"He keeps me 'cause I don't cry and whine like some of the others. I do what he wants and keep my mouth shut. It's a trade-off. I don't know where Lucas takes the girls, but I know this house. What's that saying…the devil you know or something?"

I nodded. "Yeah, I get it. How often do you work?"

She shrugged. "Four or five times a week. Isaac rotates us. It depends how many girls are in the house. And how much work he has."

"How long have you been here?"

"I don't know, a few years. It's not like we have a goddamn calendar hanging in the kitchen."

"Does he keep everybody that long?"

She shrugged. "It varies. Lucas is the travel agent," she laughed. "I sure as hell don't ask questions."

She collapsed back onto her pillow, her eyes fixed to the ceiling. "My mother was a friend of Isaac's. He used to come to our apartment and they'd get drunk and high. They'd stay in her bedroom for hours while I watched television."

"How old were you?"

"Twelve, thirteen, I don't really know. We weren't the kind of family that celebrated birthdays. I don't even think my mother knew how old I was."

"So where's your mother now?"

"Dead."

I looked at her and waited for more.

"They were in the bedroom. I was watching MTV. Isaac came out and told me she was dead and that I was coming with him. That's pretty much it. He brought me here. I worked on the farm for a couple of weeks then he brought me to the house."

"Did he, did he…?"

"Did he fuck me?"

I nodded.

"He fucks all of us."

"Why do you stay?"

"Where would I go, out into the world and get a job? I can see my resume now. Gives good head, likes being whipped. Or maybe I could go back to school. I'd have to finish eighth grade, 'cause that's where I left off. I'd fit right in, wouldn't I?"

The room got quiet. Elizabeth turned to face the wall. I listened to her breathing until it took on the slow, steady rhythm of sleep. I closed my eyes, but couldn't stop her words from repeating in my head.

OK
THURSDAY

The door opened and Rose walked into the room. "Time to get up. He wants you to put this on and come to the kitchen, now." She tossed a kimono style robe onto my bed.

"I have to shower first," I said, throwing my forearm over my eyes and blinking against the sunlight on my face.

She laughed. "You don't get it, do you? You do what he says. When he says it. And you'll be okay. You give him shit, you're gone." She jerked her thumb toward the door. "Go."

I got out of bed and wrapped the kimono around me, grateful to have something that fit. In the kitchen, Isaac sat alone at the table sipping a steaming cup of coffee. Remembering the coffee that had landed on the former house girl, I gave him a wide berth.

"Ah, Mary," he said. "Your first breakfast."

I nodded. After last night, I was barely able to look at him, let alone make small talk. I looked longingly at the coffee pot, but without knowing breakfast protocol I assumed pouring myself a cup could buy me a backhand or worse. Rose stepped into the kitchen and I exhaled.

"Get the cereal from the cupboard, put the boxes on the table. Get the milk out of the fridge. You can have a cup of coffee while you work, but you'll eat with the rest of them."

A Brady Bunch breakfast…and tonight he'll ship us out to screw his clients. Elizabeth appeared in the doorway. Isaac pulled out the chair beside him and she took it. A young girl staggered into the room on shaky legs. She'd been heavy handed at the bar yesterday and from the looks of her this morning, a shot in her coffee wouldn't hurt. Isaac glanced at her, shook his head disgusted and turned back to Elizabeth. When there were five seated around the table, Isaac cleared his throat.

"As you all know, tomorrow night we are hosting a party."

I was the only one whose head came up in response to his statement. The others continued to read the backs of the cereal boxes or stare blankly at the shapes floating in their bowls.

"I know you don't always like my parties, but they're good for business and you won't have to freeze your little asses off in the back of some schmuck's car. I have chosen the guest list carefully, only our best have been invited."

The lack of enthusiasm, except for Isaac's, made me wonder what his parties entailed. He was grinning like a Cheshire cat, the girls as solemn as undertakers.

"Rose," Isaac said, "Get things rolling."

She nodded and Isaac stood. He hesitated at the head of the table and I could feel his eyes on me. I didn't look up. My mistake. My full attention was what he wanted and I hadn't given it to him. Isaac always got what he wanted. He stepped up behind my chair, wrapped his long bony fingers around my throat and pressed the back of my head against his crotch. He bent and whispered into my ear, his breath hot on my cheek. "I haven't forgotten you. The day is young."

After Isaac went out through the back door the others began to drift from the room, but I was rooted to my seat, not trusting my legs to hold me. I nursed my coffee though my stomach threatened to send it back each time I swallowed. I tried to focus on the party instead of the feel of Isaac's penis on the back of my head. With one text to Griff I could arrange for Isaac's holiday gathering to become a surprise party with Griff and John as the uninvited guests. I might not be able to hand over Kira, but I would give them Isaac on a fucking platter.

Rose had just left the kitchen when the backdoor swung open.

"Only the dredges left, I suppose," Ruth said. She took a mug from the draining rack beside the sink and poured into it what was left in the pot before joining me at the table. "You don't look so good," she said taking a sip and grimacing at the mud in her cup.

I shrugged. "Party planning," I told her.

"Yeah. I have my list of errands." She took another sip.

"How bad are they?"

"Isaac's parties? I can't say that I've ever had the pleasure of attending one, but I've heard about them and seen the aftermath on the girls. Suffice it to say, they're not pretty."

"Violent?"

She nodded. "Isaac invites his highest paying clients, so it's not the usual guys who have a shred of conscience and need to get home to their wives and kids after a quick blowjob. It's the high rollers, a lot of cash, drugs, and with that comes the fetishes.

"The girls didn't look too pleased."

"I'm sure they're not, but it's big bucks for Isaac."

"How often does he have them?"

"Two or three times a year. Lucky you."

"I won't be…"

She raised her eyebrows. "Everyone will. Why would you be an exception? You're the new girl. They all want a taste of something new."

Her words hit my stomach like a wrecking ball. And if Isaac liked to be the first then his words about the day being young meant he'd come after me today. Once he'd had me, I was fair game for his guests. I vaguely heard Ruth talking.

"I've got to get to work," she said. "You don't look so good. Maybe you should lie down for a while."

The back door closed with a bang and I looked up to an empty kitchen. I could text Griff now to come and get me, save myself from whatever Isaac had in store and avoid the party altogether. But we'd be no further along in finding Kira than we were before. And I couldn't let the last three days be for nothing. I walked my coffee cup to the sink, poured the rest of it down the drain and started washing the breakfast dishes.

Venturing into the dark basement and hoping to avoid any squeaking, four-legged, creatures, I did two more loads of laundry. Then went back upstairs and dragged the ancient Electrolux down the hallway and pulled it into the center of the living room. No one seemed to notice me over their pipes and bottles of Jack Daniels. I used the opportunity to assess the women, filing details of each one in my head. Later, I'd pass the information to Griff. Some must have family members searching for them.

There were seven women, eight counting Rose, including myself made nine in the house, ten up until last night. Since then we'd lost the drunk girl. Like Isaac said, we were all replaceable and no doubt there'd be new ones arriving. Rose had confirmed what I already knew when she'd said that clients preferred them young. So what was I doing here? I didn't consider myself young, at least not by Isaac's definition, but he didn't know my exact age. I could pass for twenty-five if I had to. Kira had been fifteen when she left home three years ago, making her eighteen now, in her prime by Isaacs standards. I looked around the room, at a guess the current ages ranged from sixteen to early twenties.

The youngest girl was in a lacey, pink bra and panties ensemble. She had tracks on her arm and I wondered if they'd been there before Isaac had 'rescued' her. She was playing Crazy Eights with a striking blonde no more than eighteen years old with a body and a face more suitable for the cover of Vogue than this place. She had bruises around her neck in the shape of a handprint.

"Watch it."

I looked down and saw that I'd tipped over a glass. "Sorry, I wasn't looking where I was going." I pulled the handle of the vacuum back, glancing toward the door expecting a reprimand from Rose or Isaac.

"Well maybe you should." The girl got up off the couch and went to the bar to make another drink. Baby-fine, auburn curls swung across her back, but didn't hide the red welts snaking over her shoulders. They looked fresh. A few strands of her hair were stuck tight against them.

With all these young girls scattered around the room, it struck me that there was not one smile, no laughter or jokes.

Lunch was canned spaghetti. My choice since I was doing the cooking. I'm a limited chef. Lucky for me Isaac prefers processed food.

"Four girls tonight," Isaac announced coming into the kitchen while we were eating. He pointed to the ones he wanted. Elizabeth was one and I was disappointed. I'd hoped to get a chance to talk to her tonight. The other three included the girl with the welts on her back, the fingerprinted neck and one I hadn't spoken with yet.

"Your day will come," he said to me as he turned to leave the room.

Rose stayed in the kitchen as the others drifted off. She went to a cupboard and took out a bottle of bourbon. Pouring two tumblers half full she motioned for me to take one. What the hell, I thought and as the liquid stung my throat I welcomed the burn. I lifted my glass to Rose for a refill. She smiled and poured.

Ruth swung the back door wide. "Any leftovers?" she asked stepping into the kitchen.

"Shouldn't you be at the store or with the farm workers?" Rose asked.

"Store's closed midday, you know that. The women have had their break and are back to work. It's my turn now." She lowered herself into a kitchen chair.

I raised my bourbon, offering, but she shook her head.

"Coffee?"

"It's an endless pot in this house," I said and poured her a cup.

Rose was right. Ruth didn't fit. Her body was heavy and awkward made worse by combat boots and ill-fitting clothes. I wondered if she dressed that way on purpose. Her fingernails were bitten and dirty and her hair begged to be washed, but I didn't believe that she was the dimwit Rose alluded to. I think Ruth knew exactly how to keep herself on the fringes of Isaac's livelihood.

After refilling her tumbler Rose made some comment about finding better company and left the room. I sat down across from Ruth, glad to have a moment alone with her.

"Where did Lucas take the girl?" I ventured.

She took a sip of her coffee and looked at me over the rim of her cup. "Lucas runs his own business with his own contacts," she said after setting the mug back on the table.

"He sold her?"

"I guess."

"To who?"

She shrugged. "Not my problem. What'd you care?"

"I guess I'd like to know what'll happen to me if I screw-up."

"Just don't and you won't have to worry about it."

"Where's your mother?" I asked.

She looked up surprised at the question. Measured me for a moment and then said, "Gone."

"Was she…did she…live here?"

Ruth shook her head. "She left him a long time ago. I don't remember much about her."

"Why didn't she take you with her?"

She studied me again, like she was deciding on how to answer. "Didn't want me."

"I'm sorry," I said.

"Don't be."

"My mother didn't want me either, but she didn't leave. Instead she reminded me every day just how much she regretted giving birth. It would have been better if she'd left."

Ruth looked at me and nodded. "I guess we have something in common."

"What the hell are you still doing here?" Rose walked back into the kitchen.

I cursed her under my breath.

Ruth raised her cup and nodded to the bag she'd left on the counter. "Cigarettes."

"At least you're good for something," Rose said. "Isn't it time to re-open that little store of yours out in the middle of nowhere?" Rose laughed. "What do ya do all day alone, sit out back and play with yourself?"

"No Rose, that's your job."

"I wouldn't touch you with a ten foot pole."

"That's not what I meant."

"Dimwit." Rose poured herself some coffee, added a splash of bourbon and reached in the bag for a pack of cigarettes. She raised her mug. "Here's to another day in paradise."

"You don't like it, Isaac can make other arrangements."

"Fuck you," Rose said. She unwrapped the pack of cigarettes, tapped the end and drew one out between her teeth. Then she sneered at Ruth and left the room again.

"No love there, huh?" I asked.

"I don't know why he keeps that bitch around," Ruth said. "She's useless."

"She sort of watches over the girls, doesn't she?"

"Whatever." Ruth drained her mug and walked to the sink. After rinsing it, she wiped it dry and set it back in the cupboard.

"Thanks," I said.

"For what?"

"Conversation."

"No problem. I gotta get back to work." Before stepping outside her eyes met mine and I saw pity or empathy. It could have been either. It could have been both. She closed the door behind her.

After cleaning the kitchen I went upstairs to gather the sheets from the beds. I didn't work this hard at my own house, but here, housework was better than the alternative. When I stepped inside my room, Elizabeth was back in bed. I tossed the comforter from my bed to the floor. The yellow and blue floral pattern that splashed across my sheets was nothing more than a memory, the white background now a dingy gray. Creature comforts.

"I need your sheets," I said to Elizabeth.

"In a minute."

"What time did you come in last night?"

"You were awake. We talked, or were you too fucked up to remember?"

"I was fucked up but I remember. I just didn't know what time it was."

"What difference does time make?"

I tried another tactic. "Where do you go when you leave here?"

She looked at me like she didn't understand my question. "Where the fuck do you think?"

"I don't know. That's why I asked."

"You'll find out. Your turn's comin'."

"I'd like to know where I'm going before I go."

She laughed and leaned up on one elbow. "Sit down." She motioned to the end of her bed. "Once Isaac thinks you're ready, he takes you to the store."

"Bennett's Market?"

She nodded. "That's where whoever wants you picks you up. Then they bring you back after. Sometimes we don't even leave the parking lot. Just do what they want in their car, but mostly we go to a bar or a motel, occasionally to the guy's house. That's rare 'cause most of them are married."

"Does everyone always come back?"

"What'd ya mean?" She looked wary.

"I don't know. I just wondered if everyone always comes back to Isaac?" I was hoping I sounded vague enough so she wouldn't think I was fishing.

"Everyone comes back. This is where we live. If you fuck up and Isaac doesn't want you anymore then you get sold to another house and you work there."

"And that's when Lucas comes, right? When Isaac wants to sell you?"

"Why the fuck do you have to know everything?"

I pulled at the corners of the bottom sheet, afraid of pushing her too far. "I guess I'm a little scared. I want to know what's going to happen to me."

"Just don't fuck up. This is a good house. We have clothes and food, booze, pot. A lot of places aren't this good."

"Why don't any of the girls try to leave?"

"Why should they? They have more here than they had before they came. And it's a lot more than girls have at other houses."

I cringed to think of what conditions might be wherever Kira was. "Who are the men?"

"Anybody who want to get laid," she hesitated, "or whatever." Some I don't know. Some are regulars."

"Regulars from St. Bart?"

"No names, Isaac's rule."

"I won't tell him you said anything."

She looked me dead on. "I said, no names. It's Isaac's rule."

"You're loyal to him."

"He's good to me. He makes sure I get good johns. No freaks. I don't get beat-up and I don't have to do any weird shit. Just have sex and get paid. He treats me like his daughter."

Father of the year, I thought. "What about the scars on your shoulders?

"That was a one-time thing. Isaac promised never again."

"What about Ruth?"

Elizabeth laughed. "Ruth's a joke that Isaac doesn't find funny."

"What's her role in the business?"

"There isn't one. She runs the store, plays go-for, handles the farm workers and keeps her mouth shut. Isaac has as little to do with her as possible and vice versa. As far as he's concerned, I'm his daughter, not her."

I left my sheets in a pile in the middle of the room and went to gather from the other bedrooms. I'd milked all I could from Elizabeth. If I kept questioning her I ran the risk of her mentioning something to Isaac. Rose was another possibility, but I was leery of her too. Her age was already against her, she couldn't risk giving Isaac another reason to dump her if he found out she was talking.

Most of the girls were in the living room so I was surprised when I walked into a room to find someone in bed. It was the girl whose drink I'd tipped over with the vacuum, the girl with the auburn hair and welts on her back. She rolled toward me and winced as she did.

"Are you okay?" I asked.

"I need a wet cloth from the bathroom," she said. "Warm."

In the bathroom, I ran a face cloth under the hot faucet, wrung it out and brought it to her. She lay on her stomach. "Put it on my back," she said.

I lowered the blanket to her waist and groaned when I saw the welts up close. They were fresh all right, pulpy and oozing. Patches of dried blood mapped her back. "What's your name?" I asked.

"Eve."

I started to wipe it and she flinched.

"Sorry."

"Don't wipe it. Lay the cloth over my back. When it cools get another one."

"You sound like you've done this before."

"He always asks for me." She whimpered, like the child she was.

"Can't you tell Isaac what's happening?"

"He knows."

"And?"

"When I complained he said I was ungrateful. He said the client is one of his best and pays a lot for me and that he can always send me somewhere else. Someplace where I won't have it this good. The client strips me naked, beats me, and then he's done. No sex. Isaac's right. I should consider myself lucky."

Her warped assessment brought tears to my eyes and I heard myself saying the same thing to Amy twenty-five years ago. It was Christmas and I hadn't gotten the pony I'd asked for. In fact, Santa had missed our house altogether. Amy presented me with a plastic Pinto with a thick black mane and a white tail that fell past its hooves. Real or not, it was the most beautiful pony I'd ever seen. I fell asleep feeling like the luckiest girl in the world.

"Do you want something to eat?" I asked Eve. My offer sounded futile, worthless given the stakes, but I wanted to help her in some way. I wanted to take the surrender out of her eyes and relieve the pain of a girl who believed luck was getting beaten instead of raped or a plastic pony instead of a mother's love.

"Toast," Eve said. "And a glass of whiskey."

In the kitchen, I buttered the toast and carried it on a tray into the living room. I poured a tumbler half full of Jack Daniels and set it beside the plate of toast then I poured one for myself.

I set the tray down beside Eve's bed. She reached for the tumbler and downed it then picked up a piece of toast and carefully turned on her side, leaning up on one elbow. "Thanks," she said.

I gathered the sheets from where I'd left them on the floor. "I have to do the laundry,"

"Will you bring me another one when you come back?"

I took the tumbler from her outstretched hand and left her with a fresh compress on her back. But before heading to the kitchen, I took a detour into my bedroom. As I hoped, Elizabeth was gone and I grabbed the moment to text Griff. These opportunities were few and far between. I went into the bathroom and took the cell phone from its hiding place in the closet.

No info on Kira. 9 girls. One sold. "Lucas" is the middleman. Girls work at Bennett's Market. Stebbins involved. Big party Friday night. Lots of clients. Will send the details.

I added the descriptions of the three girls I'd seen earlier, and included Rose and Elizabeth asking that he check runaways and missing persons, hoping for a match. Then I told him I was safe and that I loved him. And then I threw up. Maybe it was because my body wasn't used to booze for breakfast, or because of the description Ruth had given me about Isaac's parties or because Isaac had promised to come back for me today. Maybe it was all three.

GRIFF

John's phone rang three times before Griff got an answer and then it wasn't what he'd hoped to hear.

"What," John's voice came across gruffer than usual.

"I wake you?" Griff glanced at his watch. It was three in the afternoon.

"Sort of."

"You at the precinct?"

"I'm home. You hear from Britt?"

"That's why I'm calling."

"What'd ya got?"

Griff knew from the sound of John's voice and by the fact that he was home at three o'clock on a Thursday that he was off the wagon. "You drinking?"

"A little. Tell me what you have."

"I'll tell you in person. Get in the shower."

Griff disconnected and slipped the phone into the pocket of his wool sport jacket and walked toward his SUV. He didn't have the patience right now to pick John up from a fall and he'd tell him so when he saw him.

The shower was running when Griff let himself into John's two-story cape. He stepped into the living room to wait. The room hadn't changed in years: same curtains, same furniture, and even the arrangement hadn't differed. The stack of wood in the fireplace had probably been there since Kira disappeared. He glanced at the photographs on the table beside him. Alexis looked back. John had one arm around her shoulders and the other around Kira's. They were sitting on a blanket on some sandy beach, turquoise water in the background. Kira was around ten years old in the photo.

They all looked so happy. Griff shook his head and set the frame back on the table. They had no idea that within the next six years cancer would steal Alexis, Kira would disappear and John would succumb to his demons. Griff let out a sigh. How could he blame him? But he did.

A door upstairs opened.

"Hey," Griff yelled.

"I'll be right down."

Griff picked up the bottle of Dewars from the coffee table along with the tumbler and carried them both to the kitchen. Pouring what was left in the glass down the sink drain, he looked at the bottle, debating.

"Just set it down. I'll take care of it."

Griff turned to face John. "What brought this on?"

"You did."

"Don't blame me for your decision to drink."

"I thought you were gonna pull Britt out."

"What made you think that?"

"What the hell would you have thought after our last conversation?"

"So you get shitfaced? That's your solution? No wonder you haven't found Kira." Griff regretted the statement as soon as it left his mouth.

"You're an asshole."

"I'm sorry. I shouldn't have said that."

"Damn right you shouldn't have. Where's Britt?"

"Still there. I'm not pulling her out, at least not yet."

John didn't answer. He took the bottle from Griff's hand and tucked it into an overhead cabinet then he filled the coffee pot with water and began measuring beans into the grinder. "Tell me what you've got."

"Stebbins is involved."

John turned and looked at Griff raising his eyebrows. You sure?"

Griff shrugged. "It's what Britt said. She must have seen something. It's hard to get into detail on a text. Girls are taken to Bennett's Market at night for the local's pleasure. Someone named Lucas is a middleman. It was all pretty vague, but Bennett's having a party tomorrow night. And we're going in."

"Kira?"

"Nothing yet. She did send descriptions of a couple of the other girls in the house. I'll text them to you. Maybe you can take a look at missing persons when you get to the office. I assume that's where you're heading?"

John looked at Griff. "Yeah, that's where I'm heading." He picked up a used Starbuck's to-go cup from the counter, dumped the old coffee into the sink, filled it with his fresh brew and snapped the plastic cover on.

"I'm sorry," Griff said.

"For what?"

"For making you think I was pulling Britt out. I was just upset."

John nodded and grabbed his coat off the back of a kitchen chair. "Me too."

"I need you on your game," Griff said. "We're going into Bennett's tomorrow night. You better have your head on straight."

"I hear ya," John said. "It will be. I'll get in touch with the department in Fort Kent. It'll be their shindig. We'll just be along for the ride."

"Getting Britt out of there is all I want. They're welcome to the rest of it."

"Just don't be a cowboy."

Griff glanced at John. "I'll do whatever I need to."

"Now who needs to get their head on straight?"

OK THURSDAY

I stuffed sheets and towels into the mouth of the washing machine and was just pouring in detergent when I heard the basement stairs groan. Through the dim light I saw Isaac descending and my stomach clenched.

He glanced around the dingy room. His eyes fell to the dirt floor and then rose to my face. He smiled. "Did you think I'd forgotten about you, Mary?"

My heart beat like a percussion band. I didn't answer.

He took a step toward me. I took a step back. But with the washing machine behind me, I didn't get far.

"At the party tomorrow night," he said. "It will be all my best clients. You'll be working. But I like to have my girls first before they get marked up with fingerprints or worse. Fuck me, fuck my clients, that's the order in which it goes." He laughed and came closer.

I pressed myself against the machine. I had nowhere to run.

Isaac stepped in front of me and brushed the hair out of my eyes. His gentle gesture didn't last long. He fisted the hair on the back of my head and tipped me backward over the washer.

I pulled my knee up fast between his legs. Wrong choice. His fist connected with my cheek. It flipped me sideways. I squirmed in his grasp, but he still had my hair. A chunk came out at the roots. He smacked my head onto the cover of the washing machine and held me there. I drew in a breath trying to think of a move that would set me free. But he was quicker and stronger. He flipped my body so that I was bent over the machine, the side of my face pressing against the cold, white metal.

I heard the buckle on his belt clang and then his zipper. He pulled the red kimono he'd given me to wear up over my back and rammed himself into my unwilling body.

Pine planks made up the wall behind the washing machine. Stacked edge to edge from floor to ceiling their sides splintered with tiny spikes. Nail heads penetrated two-by-fours set at eight-inch intervals. The untouched wood was veiled in dust. Spider webs stretched like gossamer over the machine's rubber hoses. The top of my head hit the dial on the washer and tears filled my eyes. I blinked them away and reverted to the scene in front of my face, anything to take me away from where I was. A long black leg emerged from between two of the boards and then another followed by a tiny head and bulbous body. The spider crept across the tapestry hunting for prey. Eight legs twitched anticipating the kill. A meal quivered on the far side of the web. The spider crept. The fly rocked and pulled futilely attempting to free itself. It's body held fast. One leg then two gripped the fly. Caught in its captor's hold diligence turned to despair and defiance became defeat.

Isaac stepped back. I reached for the kimono pulling it down over me, but I didn't move. I stared straight ahead. Words blurred in front of me, *cold, warm, hot, delicate.* I swallowed the vomit in my mouth and closed my eyes listening to him dress.

I didn't dare move until I heard his feet on the stairs and then the door to the basement closed. I sank onto the dirt floor numb and trembling my body hurt and when I looked down at my nakedness where the robe had fallen open, words like hate, repulsive and worthless came to mind. I ran my fingers over the scars on my stomach, loving them for their honesty. I should have texted Griff to come and get me. I should have told him when Isaac came after me the first time. I stood, steadying myself against the washing machine. Semen trickled down the inside of my thigh. I wiped it with the robe and started to cry. I cried so hard I could barely breathe. I was done. I was not who I'd hoped to be.

I made it up the basement stairs and across the kitchen. I started to pass the living room, but changed my mind and went to the bar. I picked up a bottle of Smirnoff, turned and headed for the stairs. I felt Rose's eyes on me and waited for her to say something about getting my work done. I wanted her to. I hesitated, even hoped, because if she had I would have smashed her head in with the bottle. At the last minute, I glanced at her. She was watching me, but didn't speak.

My bedroom was empty. I stepped into the bathroom and closed the door. I unscrewed the cap and took a long swallow then set the bottle on the floor and stood on the toilet seat. My hands shook as I slipped the phone from the top shelf in the closet. I sat down and took another swig of vodka then I texted Griff. *It's time. I need out.* I couldn't tell him why, not now. Not in a text. I sat on the toilet staring at the letters on the screen. If he came now he might miss Isaac. He wasn't always around during the day. What if he wasn't even here when they arrived? But right now I didn't really care about anything except getting myself out. I'd told Griff about the party tomorrow night. I knew he and John would see that as the best time to come. Isaac would be here with his cream of the crop clients maybe even Stebbins. I reached for the bottle, took four long swallows, draining half and wondered if I could hold out until then. The thought of staying in this house even an hour longer was unbearable. I took another sip. I couldn't come through with Kira and now my relationship with Griff was as good as over. Waiting another day seemed unfathomable, but it was the one good decision I could make after a cluster fuck of bad ones. If I sent what I'd written Griff would be here within hours. I cried as I read over my text, *It's time. I need out. Can't do this anymore. Help.* It was the truth, but if I was going to walk away from here with even a shred of dignity I'd wait until tomorrow night. I reached for the bottle and swayed as I swallowed. My right thumb hovered over SEND.

Knuckles hammered the door. I jumped and the phone slipped out of my hand. I watched in disbelief, unable to move as it skittered across the floor, under the sink and through the bent grid of the heating duct. Hearing only metal on metal as it slid through the vent into oblivion.

"What the hell are you doing in there?" Elizabeth demanded. "I gotta pee."

I picked up the Smirnoff's and stood, losing my balance my shoulder hit the wall. I reached for the latch and opened the door.

"Jesus," she said. "You see a ghost or something?" Then she pushed past me and closed the door behind her.

I sat on my bed. Had I hit SEND?

Elizabeth came out of the bathroom. "You look like hell," she said.

I didn't answer and she left me alone. I had no idea if the text was on its way to Griff or not. All I could do was wait and see if they showed up. If they did, it would be over. If they didn't…it would be over.

Rose leaned her head in the doorway. "Don't forget dinner. That's still your job."

"Fuck you, Rose," I said. Nothing mattered anymore. I was done playing the game. I had just over twenty-four hours at the most. I reached for the bottle.

"You screw up and he'll ship you out," she said.

"I've already screwed up more than you could imagine."

"Yeah? Well don't forget you've got it pretty good here. It's better than a lot of the other houses."

I stood up still holding the bottle in one hand. She was a blur in front of me. "Yeah, Rose," I said. "This is fucking awesome. Just fucking awesome."

"It's your life," she said and walked away.

I stood alone in the middle of the room, tears running down my cheeks. I started to raise the vodka to my mouth but stopped halfway and dropped the bottle to the floor. What remained of its contents soaked into the blue braided rug. I needed another kind of relief. The kind I'd used as a child to ease the pain when my mother screamed that she hated me and, why God, had she ever given birth. Why had she ever let that bastard, who was my father, near her? At those times I would go into the bathroom in the hallway on the second floor of our perfect Colonial, in our upper middle class neighborhood and run the straightedge razor that our housekeeper used to clean the bathroom grout, across my stomach. Trying to leech out my worthlessness. Warm, red blood would run down my soft pre-pubescent skin absorbed by my cotton panties and I would breathe a sigh of relief. *Go to hell,* I'd whisper to my mother.

I went back into the bathroom and opened the cabinet. There was only a pink, plastic disposable razor. I ran it across my stomach. Nothing. I held it in my fist and pressed the double steel blades as hard as I could against my skin and dragged the piece of shit across my stomach again. Warm, red blood appeared. With each passing stroke I drew more, watching as it trickled down my now adult skin and disappeared between my legs. I took a deep breath, sighed with relief. *Go to hell,* I whispered to Isaac.

OK
FRIDAY

I fought through my hangover to wake up. Remnants of the previous day drifted through my head like debris on a city sidewalk. I saw myself bent over the washing machine and swept the image aside only to have it replaced by my phone sliding across the bathroom floor, and me too drunk to react as it slipped down the broken heating vent. It had been hours since texting Griff to get me out. He hadn't arrived yet. That had to mean I'd never hit SEND, which in turn meant he wouldn't be arriving until sometime tonight. We had no plans in place regarding how he and John would come into *OK* and today when he texted me to set it up he'd get no response. How he'd react to that was up in the air. He could panic, assuming (rightfully so) that something had gone wrong and come right away or he'd wait to hear from me. The question was, how long would he wait?

The door opened. Rose stood framed in slanting rays of sun reaching through the bedroom window. "It's late. Where's breakfast? Isaac will be coming in from the cafeteria any minute. You better get your ass out of bed if you know what's good for you. You royally fucked up yesterday by not making dinner. He wasn't pleased to say the least. I'll be damned surprised if he doesn't ship you out of here today. Only thing that might save you is his party tonight. You better plan on bringing in some money."

I rolled away from her and stared at the wall. Just today, I thought. If Griff was coming then I only had to make it through today, twelve hours, fifteen at the most, but it was a big if. Head hammering and mouth so dry I thought my tongue might crack in half I swung my feet to the floor. My stomach threatened to revolt at the thought of food. I went into the bathroom, took the picture of Kira from the top shelf and slipped it into the pocket of my kimono. Kneeling on the floor, I pulled at the grate beneath the sink hoping my phone might be within reach. The cover screeched like an angry cat as I yanked it free of its metal base.

"What the fuck are you doing in there?" Elizabeth yelled from her bed, half asleep.

"I dropped something," I called back.

"Well shut the fuck up. I'm trying to sleep."

Setting the cover on the floor beside me, I lay on my stomach and slid my arm into the hole as far as I could reach, grasping and pleading, but coming up empty. The bathroom was directly above the bar. If there was a heating duct above the liquor cabinet, chances were good that my phone was sitting inside of it. There was no way I could get to it there. It was as good as gone.

The living room was empty when I crossed the threadbare Oriental rug and stepped into the alcove that housed the bar. Checking the ceiling I saw what I'd hoped I wouldn't. Running the length of the ceiling was a heating duct. There was no chance the phone could have slid all the way to the basement where I might have been able to retrieve it. It couldn't have made it past this ductwork. *Fucking stupid,* I reprimanded myself fighting back tears.

In the kitchen, struggling against my panic over losing the phone and nausea from last night, I brewed the coffee and lined up boxes of cereal on the counter. Ruth came through the backdoor at eight-fifteen as if on queue.

"Rough night?" she asked after taking a look at me.

I didn't respond. Instead I took a mug from the cupboard and poured her coffee.

"Thanks," she said. "You look awful."

Durable Goods

I sat down across from her at the table and wiped away one lone tear that hit my cheek with the back of my hand. "Your father. He called it my initiation."

She stared at the wooden surface for a minute before speaking. "I tried to warn you."

"Warn me?"

"In the store. The first day, I yelled at you to get out when he was pumping gas."

I nodded remembering. "You screamed at me, but it was because I'd dropped the bottle and made a mess."

She shook her head. "I didn't give a crap about the mess. I knew what was going to happen and I wanted you to get out before he took you."

"You were warning me?"

"Not very successfully."

"You're not loyal?"

"To that bastard? Are you kidding?"

"He's your father."

"First and foremost, he's a bastard."

"Why do you stay?"

"Where would I go? I run the store and stay out of his way."

I felt the picture in my pocket, stood and walked to the counter to get myself coffee, stalling. I should be setting the table with silverware and cereal bowls. Have bread browning in the toaster for Isaac and the girls who would soon be wandering, bleary-eyed into the kitchen looking for breakfast. But I didn't want to squander the moment. Who knew when I'd get another one and Ruth wasn't going to turn me in to Isaac, not after what she'd just said. I filled a mug for myself and returned to the table setting a plate of toast and strawberry jam between us.

"Thanks." She picked up a slice, slathering it with lumps of red jam.

I thought of the welts on Eve's back and my stomach turned then I reached into my pocket for the picture of Kira.

My hand shook as I laid it on the table in front of her and prayed that this gesture wouldn't seal my fate.

Ruth looked at it and then at me. She didn't speak.

"Have you seen her?" My words came out in a whisper though there was no one else awake yet. Ruth stared at the photo, but still said nothing. I wondered how much longer before my heart beat a hole through my chest.

She took another bite of her toast washing it down with coffee before she opened her mouth. "Why?"

"She's a friend of mine. I'm trying to find her."

"Why would you think she was here?"

"She's been missing for a long time. Her father got a postcard that he thinks was from her. It led us here."

"You cops?"

"No. Like I said she's my friend. I'm just trying to help her dad."

"Why didn't he call the cops?"

"He doesn't want trouble. He just wants to find his daughter."

Ruth finished another slice of toast and drained her mug. After pouring herself a refill, she came back and sat down. Lifting the picture in front of her face, she pursed her lips looking almost wistful. "Yeah, she was here."

I was afraid to speak, afraid of saying the wrong thing. Something that would make Ruth stop talking, walk out the door and go get Isaac. "Where is she now?"

Ruth lifted the picture again, looked at it and then at me. There were tears in her eyes. "I wish I knew," she said. She set it back on the table. "Isaac will punish me if he knows I'm talking to you like this."

"I just want to find my friend. Do you know where she is?"

Ruth shook her head. "She tried to get out, more than once. The first time she just started walking down the driveway. She was in plain sight. It was winter. She'd been out in the field cutting trees. Isaac saw her going. He called to her, but she just kept walking. I knew what he'd do so I started to run after her, to bring her back. Better me than him. But then he pulled up beside us in the pick up. I was arguing with her to turn around. He got out and hit me. He broke my nose. Then he shoved her into the truck. That's when she moved from the dormitory to the house. I didn't see her as much after that." Ruth wiped her eyes with the back of her hand.

I was getting the feeling that Kira had been more to Ruth than one of the farm workers. "Were you in love with her?"

"It was mutual."

I wondered if that was the truth or if Kira had also pegged Ruth to be the weak link and a possible way out.

"What happened after she moved to the house?"

"Her clients built fast. She was beautiful and young and…" Ruth's voice trailed off. "She was one of his best, but she was difficult. She didn't want to be here and wasn't afraid to tell him."

"When was the last time you saw her?"

Ruth sighed. "About a month ago. But Stebbins was here last week. He and Isaac were in the kitchen. Stebbins had a picture of her, said someone was looking for her. Was that you?"

"We went to Stebbins first."

"We?"

"I was with her dad and a friend."

"What'd he tell you?"

"Nothing much, but that doesn't matter. No one cares what's going on here. We just want Kira."

"When Isaac told her she was leaving, she refused. All she'd wanted since she got here was to leave and then when he told her she was, she didn't want to go. Can't blame her, you never know how much worse it'll be somewhere else. But refusing only got her a beating, a bad one. He had to wait a few days for her to heal. Clients who like bruises want to inflict them themselves, not start out with tainted goods.

Most of the girls were out with Isaac the night she left. The ones that were here were high, oblivious as usual. I went up to Kira's room. She was in bed and I lay down with her. I just held her. She liked that. She had a scrap of cardboard that she'd written *OK* on. That's all it said. On the other side was an address. She asked me to mail it for her."

"And then she left?"

"And then Isaac came into the room and saw us. He threw me across the room. I hit my head on the nightstand and was knocked out. When I woke up it was hours later, Kira was gone and the postcard was torn into pieces scattered across the floor."

"And you taped it back together and mailed it?"

Ruth nodded. A tear rolled down her cheek. "But I don't know where he took her."

"Would he have given her to Lucas?"

"Sold, you mean. They're all sold. When the locals get tired of them Isaac rotates stock. He takes farm workers he's designated for the house and moves them up or brings in new ones off the street, like he did with you. I think most of them go over the border."

"With Lucas?"

Ruth nodded.

"He sells them in Canada?"

"I'm not sure, but it's what I've overheard."

The kitchen door swung open and Isaac walked in. "What the hell are you doing here?" He checked his watch. "You got a store to run. Get moving."

I slid the picture back into my pocket and Ruth walked her coffee mug to the sink. As she passed him, he gave her a shove landing her hard against the counter. The mug fell from her hand and shattered on the tile floor. Ruth bent to pick up the glass.

"Leave it," Isaac said. "What do you think she's for?" He motioned to me, and Ruth slipped out the backdoor.

I gathered the pieces of Ruth's mug from the floor while Isaac watched. "Not for long," he said.

I sat back on my heels and looked up at him. "Not for long, what?"

"Where were you last night? Where was dinner?"

"I..." I started to explain, but he held up his hand to quiet me.

"I know where you were. Passed out."

The last thing I recalled was lying on my bed after dropping the phone. My hand went to my stomach and I winced remembering the pink plastic razor, a vice I hadn't used in years.

"I'm sorry," I said. "After...after..." I couldn't say it, couldn't say, 'after you raped me in the basement.' The words wouldn't come out of my mouth.

"I told you if you don't follow my rules then there's no place for you here." He walked to the table and picked up the plate of toast and jelly I'd given Ruth. "What's this? You fed her? Feeding the pig is not the job I gave you." He threw the plate into the sink. It smashed against the porcelain. "No dinner and now no breakfast. Was that what I asked of you?"

I shook my head.

He stood in front of me. I was still kneeling on the floor, holding the broken pieces of Ruth's mug."

"Answer me," he said.

"No," I managed.

"Good, then we understand each other," he said. Placing his boot against my shoulder, he shoved me backward.

I landed on my side and saw Rose in the doorway. Our eyes met and she smiled.

"You'll do exactly as you're told today and you'll entertain my guests tonight and then you're gone. I have no use for an ungrateful, drunken whore who can't follow the rules." He turned toward Rose. "She can leave sooner if need be."

Rose nodded.

He walked past her and disappeared down the hallway.

As soon as I heard him leave the house I went upstairs and lay on my bed condemning myself for dropping my phone. It was all I could do to focus on what needed to be done today and keep my mind off yesterday. I could fall apart once I was out of here. He'd keep me for tonight's festivities, which gave me the rest of the day to figure out what to do. I was sure that Griff and John would arrive tonight. But by the time they got here Isaac could have already sold me. If that happened I could end up over the border like Ruth said. They'd never find me. I could risk waiting to see if they showed up in time or devise an alternate plan. I was on my own.

Everyone but Rose had missed my debacle with Isaac in the kitchen so no one knew that this was my last day in the house. It would be best to keep it that way. I could hear her now, busy in the kitchen preparing food for the party. Like every other day the girls were drinking in the living room. If I tried to slip out the front door I'd be noticed. But if I offered to help Rose and she left the kitchen even for a minute, I could go out the back door, pass by the barn and make it to the tree line before anyone realized I was gone. Isaac was another matter. If he caught me, his recourse would be to beat me and sell me, but since that was the plan anyway, what did it matter. I'd rather go out belligerent than complacent.

I spent most of the morning on my bed, the girls drifted through the house in silence, but for the clinking of ice cubes in their drinks. No one shared Isaac's excitement of the impending party. As Ruth had explained, it would be a more dangerous night than usual for them because of the clientele and they were in no rush for the festivities to begin. But Isaac was becoming obsessed with the preparations. His voice rose from downstairs barking orders at Rose.

I'd almost dozed off when Rose wrapped her knuckles against my door.

"Lunch," she said. "Get it started."

I was boiling water for pasta when Ruth came in with bags of groceries.

"He's even crazier than usual," I said as she set her purchases on the counter.

"There're dollar signs in his eyes. For the most part clients are inconsistent. Some nights he gets the big money, some nights not. It depends on who wants what and when. Who's having a late night meeting, who's got business people coming from out of town, whose wife is out for the evening... Tonight, this party is by invitation only. It's all the heavy hitters."

"He mails out invitations?"

Ruth laughed. "Word of mouth. He has his mules. Two legged ones."

I went to the counter and began emptying the bags Ruth had brought. There was a shrimp platter with cocktail sauce in the center, a plate with an assortment of cheese and crackers, marinated mushrooms and meatballs. My stomach churned.

"Put everything in the fridge," Rose said sweeping into the room, a cigarette clamped between her teeth. "I'll handle serving and arrangement. You just unpack."

She turned to Ruth. "Where's the booze?"

"I have to go pick it up."

"Then what are you doing standing here? Go." She shooed her away with a flick of her hand.

Ruth glanced at me and rolled her eyes. "Back in a couple of hours," she said.

"Are you coming to the party?" I asked.

"Not a chance," she said and closed the door behind her.

"Get this stuff put away," Rose said and went into the hallway. The vacuum roared to life.

I placed the last item, a bottle of Tabasco sauce, on the counter and folded the empty bag. Something rattled inside and I opened it to see what I'd missed. At the bottom, lying against the brown paper was the watch Griff had given me. The one that I'd told Ruth was my mother's when she'd taken it away that first day at the dormitory. I lifted it out and hugged it to my chest, overwhelmed by the emotions it triggered. I was getting out tonight, one way or another. I slipped the watch over my hand and pushed it high on my forearm hidden under the flimsy satin sleeve of my robe.

"If you're finished putting things away, go upstairs and put some make-up on," Rose said coming into the kitchen. "I'll finish here."

I felt sick as I turned to do as I was told. I climbed the stairs and felt the watch on my arm. Very soon it would all be over, one way or another.

Elizabeth was in the bathroom leaning over the sink, a wand of mascara in one hand and a bottle of Jack Daniels in the other.

"Starting a little early aren't you?" I asked.

"Fuck-off," she said. "Like you should talk."

"So tonight's the big night?"

She turned to look at me. "Lots of money, important people. We don't have to sit in some dick's car and freeze our asses off. Tonight they come to us."

"Isn't a john, a john?"

She took a slug from the bottle. "Not always. Tonight it won't be just anyone who has fifty bucks."

"Ruth said the more they have to spend, the more they want the unconventional."

"Ruth doesn't know shit."

"The girls don't seem too excited."

Elizabeth shrugged. "Isaac tries to pair us up with who we deserve."

I lay back and looked at the ceiling wondering who would be coming through Isaac's door and if any of them would be leaving in the back of a police cruiser.

"It's all yours," Elizabeth said coming out of the bathroom. She walked to the closet and selected a turquoise halter-top slit to the waist and a short, white leather skirt.

I'd never been much for make-up and had no experience with the array of products Rose had supplied. Give me a lipstick and mascara and I was good to go, but in the bag before me lay an array of eyeliners, eye shadows, blush and concealers that I had no idea how to apply. Seeing my quandary, Elizabeth laughed.

"You need help?" she asked.

"If you have the time."

She did my make-up, tossed a black silk mini skirt and silver sequined tank top on the bed and took a pair of black patent stilettos from the closet. In fifteen minutes, she had me looking like I belonged there. I wasn't sure if that was a good thing or not. But Isaac seemed pleased when we came downstairs dressed and ready for whatever the evening would bring. I followed her to the bar and accepted the shot of Smirnoff's she handed me. A little fortification might counteract the adrenalin ricocheting through me.

By six-thirty everyone had a heavy buzz on board. Even Isaac had come in early from the barn and downed a couple of shots, a rarity. He was upstairs changing out of his work clothes. In the living room, the girls were subdued. Rose was rattling around in the kitchen like a pretentious hostess. Since most of the food Isaac had bought was pre-cooked and pre-arranged on platters, she was doing little more than moving plates around the counter.

"What do you want?" she asked when I came into the room interrupting her fantasy.

"Do you need any help?"

She laughed. "A little late for that don't you think? You'll be gone tonight." She untied her apron and tossed it onto the counter. "I need to change my clothes. I've been stuck in this kitchen all day."

The martyr, I thought. "I'll keep an eye on things out here. Go ahead," I said, seeing my moment materialize.

"I won't be long. Keep the girls out of here." She disappeared up the back staircase.

It had to be now. There was nothing I needed to take from this place. I opened the backdoor and under a dim watted bulb slipped outside onto the porch, down the steps and across the side yard toward the barn. The only other light was on the front of the house illuminating the driveway. At the barn I stopped and leaned against the outside of the far wall, listening. Nothing. I was shaking from fear or the frigid air, either way I had to keep moving. I slipped the watch out of my shoe and onto my wrist, then headed for the trees. Two feet from the pines, I heard the backdoor slam. I dove into the shadows, tearing the skin on my forearms as I brushed heavy pine boughs out of my way. I could still barely make out the back door. Isaac was coming down the steps. He wasn't moving fast. He seemed to be looking for something on the ground. He stooped, picked up a bucket and went back inside.

I held onto the tree beside me until my breathing returned to normal and my heart slowed, but I couldn't wait for long. Sooner or later Rose would be back in the kitchen asking where I was. I took off running deeper into the woods. The moonlight was both a blessing and a curse. The driveway was to my right and if I stayed in a straight line parallel to it, I'd eventually reach the road. But ducking branches and avoiding fallen trees had me unsure if I'd veered off course. I stopped again to listen. It was dead still around me and with a mix of crusty snow and brittle leaves underfoot there'd be no way anyone could sneak up. I took off again but didn't get more than ten feet when I tripped over an exposed root and went down hard. A sharp pain shot through my forearm and I couldn't move my wrist. Struggling to my knees, I wrapped my right hand around my left wrist holding it tight against my chest. The watch from Griff was gone. The clasp must have broken in the fall. There was no time to search for it. Back on my feet I was running again. I'd completely lost my bearings and didn't know if I was still moving in the direction of the road or back toward the house. It was slower going having to hold my arm and the jolt of each step increased the pain.

Ahead of me, through the trees there was a light. I stopped and watched. If it moved, it meant I'd reached the road. If not, I was back at the house. It moved toward me and became two. It was headlights. A car was coming. I felt delirious and forgetting the pain in my arm, ran headlong toward the road. I had to reach the car before it passed.

I stepped onto the road and waved my good arm moving as far toward the center of the hot top as I dared. The car came to a stop in front of me and I bent forward at the waist ready to collapse. Tears of relief poured down my cheeks. The driver's door opened and a man stepped out. As he came toward me I recognized Sheriff Stebbins.

"Well, well, well, don't you look all banged up. Come outta them trees, huh? What're ya runnin' from? A bear?" He started laughing and looked me up and down. "I know where you belong and lucky for you I'm heading your way. Bet Isaac will be damn pleased to see who I'm bringin' home. Don't you think?"

He grabbed my arm and pulled me to the cruiser, opened the back door and threw me in. Once in the driver's seat, Stebbins hit a button and all four locks clicked into place.

My arm throbbed, but I could move my wrist. Not broken. I leaned back against the seat. Stebbins had met me before, but he didn't seem to remember. That might change once we got inside Isaac's house and he saw my face in the light.

Stebbins pushed me through the door ahead of him. Isaac was standing in the doorway of the living room. The look on his face when he saw me was what I'd like to call priceless, but that would indicate that I found even the slightest bit of enjoyment in the moment. I didn't. He took a step toward me and the next thing I knew, I was on my knees from a backhand I'd never seen coming.

"You're gone," he said. "Tonight. And what I'll recommend for you will make you regret every minute of your insolence."

He stepped forward and raised his hand again.

"Hold on, hold on," Sheriff Stebbins said putting his hand against Isaac's arm. "She might as well earn you something before she goes."

A slow smile spread across Isaac's mouth. "And I know just the client. Go clean yourself up." He nodded to Rose who was hovering in the hallway. "Go with her. Watch her."

I stood and moved toward the stairs.

"Wait a minute," Stebbins said. He took my elbow and turned me to face him. "Don't I know you? You look awful familiar now I'm gettin' a good look."

I shook my head. "I've never seen you before. I'd remember your pencil dick."

He sneered, but I could see the wheels turning. I had a limited amount of time before they clicked into place.

In the bathroom I ran cold water over my wrist and held a cloth to my cheek then I sat on the toilet and wiped dried blood from the scratches on my knees and shins. I wanted to lie down and cry, but giving in to my desperation only made it more real.

Terror doesn't come close to describing my feelings as I followed Rose down the stairway. If Stebbins remembered where he'd seen me Isaac would erupt realizing a raid was imminent. The doorbell rang and Rose went to answer it. I tried to blend into the furniture while I watched the girls travel up and down the stairs with an array of clients on their arms, sometimes two at a time. I glanced out the window and prayed for headlights. Someone sat beside me and I turned to see Rose.

"Hiding?" she laughed and sucked hard on the cigarette between her lips.

I didn't answer.

"That was a stupid move," she said. "You'll pay."

"Do you know these men?" I asked wanting to change the subject. I couldn't think about what was coming if Griff didn't show soon.

"Most of them," she said. "They're Isaac's elite."

"From St. Bart?"

She pointed to a bearded, broad shoulder guy leaning across the bar toward Elizabeth. "That's Dr. Roth. He takes care of STDs, birth control, even unwanted pregnancies when they occur. It's rare but it happens." Next she nodded toward a rail thin man sucking on a cigar, his eyes shifting constantly around the room. "That's our Chief of Police."

"Stebbins."

"You know him?"

"Not until tonight," I said hoping it was a smooth recovery.

She nodded and started to point out another, but Dr. Roth stepped in front of us and blocked our view.

"Rose," he said pulling her to her feet. "How about getting the old doc a drink and maybe a little something else?" He curled his palm over her butt and propelled her toward the bar. Had they been anywhere else they would have looked like an ordinary couple.

I glanced again out the window yearning for headlights. When I turned back to the room Isaac stood in front of me. He lifted me by my hair until I was standing in front of him. "Another drink?"

He took my elbow and steered me to the bar. Stebbins looked up and studied my face. I turned away from him. Isaac grabbed the Smirnoff's and topped off my glass. "I have someone I want you to take care of," he said. "Come with me."

I followed him from the living room down the hall and into the kitchen where a different sort of party was going on. A couple of the girls were naked and dancing on top of the kitchen table, slow and evocative, running their hands over their breast and between their legs. Elizabeth was straddling a fat, bald guy. Her white leather skirt hiked up around her waist. She rocked back and forth on top of him while he sucked on a cigar and watched the girls dance.

Eve lay at the foot of the back stairway. Blood dripped from a gash on the side of her head onto the tile floor. Isaac lifted her by one arm and propped her against the wall. She pressed her palm above her ear then studied her hand as though it was something foreign. Dabbing at the rivulets on her cheekbone, she smeared the blood like a drunken face painter.

"Sorry for the problem, Edward," Isaac said pushing me toward the man who stood at the foot of the stairs. "I have something else for you."

The man Isaac spoke to was dressed in a suit, an ascot in his pocket and a gold pinky ring on each hand. His hair was dark and thick and slicked back over his head except for one stray, greasy strand that hung above his right eye.

"Something special, Edward. Something very special and almost untouched." He winked.

Edward took a step toward me and slid his eyes over my body. "She'll do."

I raised my glass and drained it. The tinkling ice cubes betrayed my shaking hand. This was Eve's guy, the one who left welts. He took hold of my elbow and led me up the back stairs and into a room. It was the same one I'd been in with Isaac. I wanted to pull away and tell him he'd made a mistake. I wasn't one of them. I could promise to get him out of there before the cops showed up. Could he keep a secret? I weighed my options.

"Take off your clothes," he said.

As slowly as I could, I undressed. He seemed to like my lack of hurry, assuming it was purposeful and that I was building his anticipation. But I was stalling, waiting to hear the door burst open downstairs, waiting to be saved. If I offered this guy an out and Griff never showed up, he'd tell Isaac and I was as good as dead. I dropped my lace thong onto the floor.

Edward looked me over. I wondered if he noticed the make-up on my stomach, hiding the scars. Maybe he'd return me to Isaac as damaged goods. But as I waited, hoping, he removed a whip from his pocket. The kind an animal tamer might use in a circus act, long and thin. He snapped it a couple of times in the air in front of my face. I thought of Eve. I thought of Griff. And I thought I was lucky to be getting whipped and not raped.

"Turn around," he said.

I lost track of how many times the whip connected with my back. Each time it did, Edward's breathing got harder and faster. A waterfall of tears fell onto the oriental carpet beneath me. I fell onto my side and curled into a fetal position. The whip caught my cheek and I raised my arm.

"Stop," my voice cracked barely above a whisper.

"Get up." Edward stepped toward me. As he did the door opened.

"Get up." It was Isaac's voice. "I said get up." He reached down and pulled me to standing by my elbow. His face was inches from mine. "Stebbins remembered where he saw you. You're a fucking cop." He shoved me hard. I landed on the floor and he kicked the side of my thigh with the toe of his cowboy boot.

"I'm not a cop," I said grabbing my leg.

"Shut up and get your clothes on, now."

"Edward," he said, "Get on your way."

Edward said nothing and left the room.

I reached for my sequined tank top and slipped it over my head. The slightest movement brought searing pain across my back and the thin fabric of the shirt stuck tight to my bloodied skin. I fought the urge to be sick and stood, pulling the pink thong up my thighs. I zipped the black silk skirt in place and then looked at Isaac.

"I'd like to fucking kill you right now," he said. He grabbed me by the throat and pushed me against the wall. "When are they coming?"

"I don't know," I managed as he tightened his grip.

"You know." He smacked my head against the wall."

"Tomorrow," I said. "They're coming tomorrow.

He threw me out into the hallway and I slammed into the wall.

"Get downstairs."

The house was empty except for one man who stood framed in the open front door. He was handsome in that lean, chiseled, five o'clock shadow way, wearing tight, black jeans and a black leather jacket. Jet-black hair was combed back from his face and he was one hell of a cut above Isaac. I cursed myself for even registering his good looks and scanned the living room. It was empty. Everyone was gone, even the girls. Isaac must have cleared them out after Stebbins remembered who I was.

"This is Lucas," Isaac said. "You're going with him." He wrapped his palm around the back of my neck and threw me toward the open door. "Get the fuck out of my house."

My cheek connected with the narrow edge of the open front door and I staggered back from it, holding my face. My breath caught in my chest. "I can't," I said. "I promise…"

Isaac took my elbow and shoved me through the doorway onto the front porch. He stepped toward me raising his arm ready to give me one last blow.

Lucas stopped him. "Enough. You're messing up my merchandise." He took my arm and led me toward the stairs.

I stared down the driveway willing Griff's headlights into being, but nothing broke the darkness. In Lucas' BMW I huddled against the door and watched in the rearview mirror as the lights faded behind us and we drove away from the house, the girls, the dormitory, Sarah and Ruth, away from my picture of Kira and my cell phone buried inside it all. We'd driven two or three miles up the road when a string of police cars passed us, lights flashing, sirens blaring. Griff was on his way to get me out and I was within six feet of him, heading in the opposite direction.

GRIFF

Ahead of them, a pick-up veered across the frozen pasture to their right. The two cruisers out front continued up the driveway toward the house.

"Follow the truck," Griff said. "That's Bennett."

"You sure?" John asked.

"I remember it from the market when he picked up Britt."

Officer Damon from the Fort Kent PD pulled the steering wheel hard and the cruiser swerved off the driveway and onto the snowy ground in pursuit. The car bounced over a mix of terrain. Frozen mud, snow and potholes made from pawing hooves sent the cruiser bouncing and sliding over the rough ground making their pursuit feel more like a carnival ride than a chase.

"We blow a tire, we're screwed," Damon said.

"Then don't let it happen," John answered.

The cop rolled his eyes, but kept up his not too shabby driving.

Ahead of them Isaac plowed through a barbed wire fencing, dragging wooden poles alongside his truck. In front of him stood a wall of trees.

"He's got nowhere to go," John said. "He's gonna turn back this way."

Isaac's truck skidded into a three hundred and sixty degree turn and came to a stop, hesitating like a bull sizing up his matador. Then he gunned it, heading straight for them.

"Looks like he wants a game of chicken," Griff said.

"This guy's messin' with the wrong opponent." Damon grinned. "I was the king of chicken in high school."

"Don't know if I'm happy about that or not." John clicked his seat belt into place.

Isaac was driving directly toward them, his speed steadily increasing. Damon did the same, not taking his eyes off the truck. They were fifty feet from each other, thirty…twenty…

"Hold on," Damon said and slammed his foot down on the brake turning the steering wheel hard to the right causing the tail end of the cruiser to fishtail left. The car slipped and slid, skidding sideways over the frosty ground, coming to a stop just as the F-150 rammed them broadside.

Griff was out of the cruiser before the engine died running toward the truck. He ripped open the front door and pulled a half conscious Isaac out by the collar, punching him in the face before dropping him onto the frozen ground.

"What the fuck?" Isaac said, dazed.

Griff bent over, lifted him by his coat collar and held a picture of Britt in front of his face. "She in your house?"

Isaac shook his head and winced. "Never seen her."

Griff planted another one on his right cheek, splitting it open before letting him fall to the ground again.

"Not the game to play with me," Damon said looking at Isaac as he came up beside Griff.

Isaac Bennett lay at their feet curled in fetal position. "Get me an ambulance," he mumbled.

"Fat chance." John knelt beside him and showed him a picture of Kira. "Where is she?"

Isaac closed his eyes and didn't answer.

John grabbed a handful of hair yanking his head back.

A cry escaped Isaac's lips.

"I said have you seen her?"

"No," he whispered. "Never. Now get me an ambulance."

A squad car pulled alongside Damon's crushed cruiser.

"Looks like you could use a ride."

The two cops pulled Isaac to his feet and threw him into the back of the car locking the doors.

"You find anything at the house?" Griff asked the cop.

"No warm bodies, but plenty of shit pointing to a small prostitution enterprise."

Griff glanced across the field. A group of twenty or more women were being escorted from the dormitory building up the driveway toward Isaac's house and the police vans that had arrived out front.

"They're not here,' Griff said to John. "Neither one of them."

"But they were," John said. "We were that close." He held up his thumb and forefinger.

"Close doesn't bring them home."

"But close is a fucking lot better than what I've had for the past three years. We'll find them."

"You two want a ride?" Damon asked over his shoulder as he and the other cop walked toward the cruiser with Bennett in the backseat.

"We'll walk," Griff said and he and John began their trek across the frozen pasture toward the house.

"What if Bennett doesn't talk?" John asked.

Griff looked down at the bloody knuckles on the back of his hand. "He will."

CANADA
FRIDAY

I couldn't be sure how much time had passed. I'd dozed off for what might have been a minute but could have been an hour. The pain emanating from my back dulled all other senses, physical and emotional. I didn't fight it. Numb was where I wanted to be. The only road sign we'd passed was for Madawaska, but I wasn't sure if I'd seen it or dreamt it. I kept fading in and out. There was a border crossing there and it could be where we were headed unless Lucas had his own personal backdoor. We were travelling down a one-lane highway. It was dark and tree-lined. The only lights came from logging trucks roaring past, thousands of pounds strapped to their back. When I was young, I was afraid of those trucks. What if the cinch let go and a multitude of limbs and trunks rolled onto the car I was in? I leaned my head back against the seat thinking that I would welcome that end now. *Snap*, I willed each one as it past.

In the headlights a Border Crossing came into view and a sign for Edmundston. Lucas began to slow the car. This could be my chance for escape, my only chance. They would ask our business in Canada and want to see my passport. What would he show them?

Lucas stopped beside the guardhouse and a uniformed officer stepped up to his window. There was a gun hanging from his belt. I closed my eyes and relaxed. This man would want information that Lucas couldn't give. I was about to be freed.

"Ahh, Lucas," the guard said.

My eyes flew open and I turned my head to see the two men shaking hands through the window.

"Alain, how goes it with you tonight?" Lucas asked.

"Very well and you too I hope?"

"Yes, yes. Returning from a party. A very nice evening."

"Glad to hear it, sir."

Alain stepped back and waved us through.

"Wait," I said straightening up as best I could. I winced as I peeled my oozing back from the leather seat. I wasn't letting this chance slip by.

Lucas looked at me annoyed. Alain bent and looked through the window past Lucas to me. "Yes, Mademoiselle? A smile played across his face.

"I have to go to the bathroom."

I turned to Lucas. "Can we stop, please?"

"Inside, to your right." Alain pointed toward the building.

Lucas grunted and turned the car into the lot, parking in front of the building to our left. A sign over the door read, Welcome Visitors.

He took me by the elbow and steered me inside to the ladies room. There were no windows above the stalls as I'd hoped. No windows at all. I glanced into the mirror, recoiling at what I saw. One side of my face, the side that had connected with Isaac's hand and the front door, was the color of a summer sunset. My eye was already swollen shut and my cheek puffed to twice its normal size. I started to touch it, thought the better of it and dry heaved into the sink. I couldn't bear to think of how close Griff and John had been. Another ten minutes and we'd have had Isaac and Lucas in handcuffs and I'd be riding home beside Griff, safe and sound and somewhat successful.

I rinsed my mouth and splashed cold water onto my face gently blotting it with a scratchy paper towel. They'd have no clue where I was unless Isaac talked and I didn't think there was much chance of that. Unless Ruth stepped up with information it would be tough for Griff and John to press charges against Isaac. I hung my head over the sink and let the tears come. They ran over my cheeks, stinging the pulpy skin around my eyes. I'd wanted to hand over everything, Kira, Isaac, Stebbins and the rest of them and instead I'd given them an empty house. I looked in the mirror, groaning at the sight of myself and looked away. There was no Amy here to swoop in and fix things. No Griff. It was up to me. I took a breath. *"Get your shit together. It's not over yet. There's a way out. Find it."*

I remembered passing an office on the way to the bathroom. There'd been a man inside at a desk and a telephone on the desk. I opened the bathroom door a crack. If I could just get to the office without Lucas seeing me, I could tell the man at the desk what was happening. I leaned my head into the hallway. There was no sign of Lucas. Stepping out of the ladies room I ran to the office pulled the door open and stepped inside. The man turned his head and looked at me. "Can I help you, mademoiselle?" the man asked.

From the corner of my eye I caught a glimpse of someone else in the room.

"She's with me," Lucas said stepping forward and taking my arm. "Have a good one, Charles." He guided me through the door and back outside to the car.

Once we were in the car and out of view of the men inside he punched me. My neck snapped and my head hit the window. "Don't be stupid," he said. "I have no time to babysit. You do what I tell you or you become trash. You know what I do with trash?".

I shook my head, wincing from the pain.

"I crush it with my hands and toss it in the nearest Dumpster. Are we clear?"

"Yes," I whispered trying not to move my jaw.

"Good," He pulled the car onto the road and we travelled in silence.

I wondered why Lucas had bought me, considering my identity and the risk that posed. But maybe Isaac hadn't told him who I was. That would make sense. Isaac had found one last way to make money off me. But selling me to Lucas and neglecting to mention that I was a PI with a connection to the Portland PD was no small oversight. And one I hoped he'd pay for.

I leaned my head against the seat, closed my eyes and wondered what was happening with Griff and John right now. Were they at Isaac's? Were they walking through the rooms I'd just left? Was Griff standing in the bedroom I'd shared with Elizabeth? Could he feel my presence? Was he in the room where Edward had whipped me? Did he know the blood on the floor was mine? Griff had seen something worthwhile in me when he'd asked me to be a partner in his firm. But now, every time he took me in his arms, he'd feel my scars beneath his hands and we'd both remember where I'd been and what Isaac had done to me. I'd failed Griff and John and Kira and all the women at Isaac's.

GRIFF

The house reeked of booze and cigarettes. Glasses and bottles littered every surface and clothes lay strewn across bedroom floors. Around them lab techs dusted for prints. Gloved cops opened drawers and emptied closets. Griff and John walked shoulder to shoulder in silence taking it all in. Griff's jaw tight, John's fists clenching and unclenching. Imagining the hours, the days, the unbearable minutes Britt and Kira had endured here. At the same time blocking the images from their minds so not to be consumed by their own guilt.

At the top of the stairs Griff pulled out his cell phone, opened the Find My Phone app and keyed in Britt's number.

"Wasn't she keeping the phone turned off?" John asked.

"Maybe she forgot. Maybe wherever she is, she just turned it on. Maybe it'll show me something. What the hell else have we got?"

John didn't answer. The truth was, they had nothing. If Bennett didn't talk they'd have no way of locating Britt."

Griff's phone pinged and he zeroed in on the blue dot on the screen.

"What's it say?" John leaned over his shoulder to get a look at the phone.

"It's here. The phone is in the house and it's on." Griff looked at John. "Maybe Britt is too."

"Hiding?"

Griff shrugged. Hurrying down the stairs he found Sergeant McCullem of the Fort Kent PD. He held up his cell phone. "My partner's phone is in the house. I don't know if that means she is too."

"Start in the basement," McCullem instructed two cops in the hallway. "Work your way up. We're looking for a cell phone or its owner, Britt Callahan."

Griff and John trampled down the basement steps behind the two officers. They tore apart the dank farmhouse cellar while Griff called Britt's cell.

"Hey," a voice called down the stairs, "We've got a vibration coming from the ceiling over the bar. Could be the phone."

Griff took the steps two at a time. When he got to the living room a cop was standing on the bar stabbing a screwdriver into the drywall ceiling.

"Try this," a lab tech handed him a crowbar he'd taken from one of the cars outside.

The cop rammed it into the drywall pulling down a large square of the ceiling and exposing a metal heating duct. "Call it again," he said to Griff.

The duct vibrated and the cop slammed the crowbar against its seam. The thin aluminum crinkled and split. The vibrating phone dropped onto the bar. Griff grabbed it, stopped the call and went to the messages screen. He read Britt's last text aloud. *It's time. I need out. Can't do this anymore. Help.* He looked to see when it was written. Thursday night.

"She never hit SEND," he said staring at the phone. "What the fuck. Why didn't she...I would have..."

"Bag that," Sergeant McCullem nodded toward the cell phone in Griff's hand. Reluctantly, Griff dropped the phone into the plastic evidence bag a young cop held in front of him. Then he stepped out of the alcove and drove his fist through the living room wall.

CANADA
SATURDAY

The digital clock on the dashboard read two-forty five when we pulled into a small town and began making a series of turns down narrow streets, finally stopping outside a three-story brick apartment house. An ancient, rusted out fire escape scaled the back of the building providing small landings outside the second and third floors.

"Get out," Lucas said. "Follow me."

I stepped from the car, shivering in the cold. I had nothing with me except what I'd been wearing at Isaac's. A row of houses stretched down either side of the street. We walked up five metal stairs. I shook beside him as he shoved his key into the lock on the front door of the nondescript building. Releasing it, he followed suit with two more and pushed the door open. A narrow hallway stretched before us, a Tiffany style lamp on a small round table lit the way.

"Get inside," he said and shoved me into a darkened room.

A fist I never saw coming connected with my cheek and knocked me to the floor.

"This is how we do business here," said a voice I didn't recognize. "From what I hear, Isaac treats his girls too good. Here, whores get what they deserve."

I struggled to my feet. The only light came from the lamp in the hallway. Lucas stood in the doorway, watching. Out of the shadows to my left a man emerged.

"She's all yours, Clive," Lucas said. The man handed Lucas an envelope. Without a word Lucas left the room and I heard the front door close.

Clive stood for a moment his gaze frozen on the doorway as though making sure that Lucas was gone. Dark, curly hair brushed against his flannel collar. His profile was gaunt. Protruding cheekbones flanked a beaked nose and his shirt sagged against a hollow stomach. He looked more like a scarecrow than a businessman. Once satisfied that Lucas was gone, he came toward me, balled his left hand and planted it in my stomach. I folded at the waist and landed on my knees.

"Let's go," he said and pulled me up with his hand in my armpit then pushed me into the hallway. I winced at the pressure of his hand against the torn flesh on my back. We stepped into a kitchen and he unlocked a door to my left, a stairway led to the basement. The light was dim and the smell rank, he followed me down the stairs. As my eyes adjusted I could make out bodies. Six mattresses lined the floor. A low watt, overhead light bulb shed what little light there was in the room. I could see my breath. He stepped up to one of the mattresses and kicked the shape beneath the blanket. "Move over," he said. Obediently, the shape complied. "Lie down." He pointed to the vacated space.

I lay on the mattress and pulled one side of the blanket over myself and up to my chin. Without another word he walked to the stairs in the corner of the room. I listened until he'd reached the top then he closed and locked the door behind him. The person beside me shifted and rolled toward me. We looked at each other without speaking. Even in the shadows of the basement I could see the sallow color of her skin and the sunken depths below her eyes.

"I'm Julia," she whispered as though desperate for me to know she had a name. Beneath the blanket she took my hand and held it in both of hers. I closed my eyes and fell asleep.

SATURDAY

When I woke up it was to the sound of feet coming down the stairway. The room was no brighter than it had been the night before. There were no windows to announce the morning or welcome a ray of sun. No windows to let escape the rank air heavy with the musty scent of sex. Clive stood on the bottom step with a paper bag in one hand and a plastic container of orange juice in the other. "Breakfast," he said and set both on the floor then he turned and retreated.

I couldn't remember the last time I'd eaten. Maybe it had been lunch in Isaac's kitchen the day before with Ruth. I wondered what she'd tell police, or had she escaped out of the dormitory before they'd reached her? She hadn't done anything when he'd sold Kira, and she'd been in love with her. It was a waste of time to hope she'd do something for me. I rolled to my knees and stood, wincing. The skin on my back cracked open with the slightest movement. Not knowing the protocol in my new home, I was afraid of making a wrong move, but hunger won out. I walked to the stairs careful to avoid the mattresses and uncurled the top of the bag. I pulled out a sesame bagel and bit into heaven. Unscrewing the lid on the orange juice, I washed it down and sat back on my heels feeling the nourishment hit my stomach. Someone came up beside me and pulled the bag toward them and I crawled back to my mattress clutching the bagel to my chest like a dog guarding a bone.

The bag made its way from one hand to the next until it was empty, the OJ followed suit. I tried to savor each not knowing when I'd eat again. I looked at Julia. She'd held my hand for most of the night. I wasn't sure if it was for my comfort or her own.

"Where are we?" I asked her.

She shrugged. "I don't know for sure. It was dark when he brought me here. I was high. I remember seeing a sign that said Grand Falls, but I don't know if that's where we are now. When we go to the bar we don't pass any street signs."

"The bar?"

"Rusty's, it's where we work."

"How did you end up here?"

She took a bite of the bagel in her hand and kept her eyes on the blanket as though deciding how to answer. Finally, she looked up. "My boyfriend sold me." Her eyes fell away from mine ashamed.

"Your boyfriend sold you?" I heard the disbelief in my tone and felt stupid for letting my naïveté show.

"I was at a party. He introduced me to Lucas and Lucas handed him a roll of money. I didn't think anything of it at the time. Stupid me. When Lucas said he was going out to score and asked me to go with him, I went. He brought me here. That's what the money exchange was about, but at the time I didn't understand."

"How long ago was that?"

"I don't know any more."

"Where are you from?"

"Presque Isle."

"Did you cross at Edmundston?"

She nodded.

There were border crossings closer in proximity to Presque Isle, but I remembered Lucas' handshake with Alain, the guard. Stebbins and Isaac were feeder fish and I was moving up the chain.

"Who's Clive?" I asked Julia.

"This is his house. We work for him."

"And Lucas?"

"A middleman, I think. He handles sales and transports."

"What about your boyfriend? Is he involved?"

"I haven't seen him since that night."

"Does Clive treat you...us, okay?"

She laughed a tired laugh. "Do I look okay?" She raised one arm and motioned to the other girls. "Do they?"

I looked around the room. Dead, listless eyes looked back, youth long gone, but ages were impossible to estimate.

"He treats us like dogs," one of the woman said. "Worse. They screw us and beat us and then hand us their scraps."

"Stop your whining." A woman in the corner said. "You could have it worse."

The woman reminded me of Rose and I had a sudden longing to be back at Isaac's. Rose had told me I could have it a lot worse and she'd been right.

"Louise, you think this is good, because you were on the street. You were already a whore. But the rest of us had lives." Julia looked at me and rolled her eyes. "Don't listen to her."

"Well la-ti-da,' Louise said. "Ain't you the woman of the house."

A small form beneath a blanket in the far side of the room whimpered.

"Where's the bar? Rusty's?" I asked Julia. I'd been ready to give up in the bathroom at the crossing, but with no way to contact Griff and Stark if I gave up now, this would be my life. One way or another, I was getting home.

"I'm not sure where it is. A long dark road is the only thing we ever see. It's a dive bar. Clive and Myles take us in a van."

"Who's Myles?"

"Clive's partner." She tucked a strand of stringy brown hair behind her ear. "We have sex with the clients and sometimes we get food. French fries. A burger if we're lucky. When they're done with us Clive and Myles bring us back. This is home." She laughed. "Home sweet home."

The door at the top of the stairs opened.

"Thought you were something special, did you?" It was a new voice. "See what you get when you question my authority? I paid for you. I own you. But now little bitch, I'll send you out with the rest of them. No more special treatment."

A woman was crying. "No. Please. I'll do--"

"You'll do whatever I tell you to do, whore," he said.

A blur of limbs and blond hair came tumbling down the stairs head over heels. When she landed at the bottom, he laughed and closed the door. Above us the lock clicked into place.

Julia crawled over the mattresses to the young woman. "Bastard," she said.

I followed her. "Who was that?"

"Myles. He likes to keep one of us for his own personal use from time to time. He thinks he's doing us a favor. But he's fucking sick, deranged. I'd rather screw ten guys at the bar than spend one night with him."

Julia reached the bottom of the stairs and sat back on her heels looking at me. "The stuff he makes us do." Her eyes dropped to her lap while she played some scene in her mind. She shook her head and looked up. "Don't ask. Just pray he never wants you."

She slipped her hands beneath the girl's armpits and I took her ankles. Together, we dragged her back to our mattress, straightened her body, slipped off her shoes and pulled a blanket up to her chin. I brushed the girl's dirty blond hair away from her face and looked down at Kira.

While Kira slept, I imagined what I'd say to her when she woke up. We'd met a few times when Griff and I first started dating. Kira had been about twelve. I'd spoken with her briefly at her mother's funeral and hadn't seen her since, so it wasn't like she'd recognize me the minute she opened her eyes. Both of which were swollen shut. The deep purple spheres around them looked more like a Halloween mask than a young woman's skin. Her lips were puffy and cracked. A rivulet of dried blood trailed from her nose to the corner of her mouth.

"How long was she with Myles?" I asked Julia.

"He took her three or four days ago. She's been here for about a month, I think. It's hard to judge time."

Ruth said that Isaac had sold Kira to Lucas about a month before I arrived at the farm. So if both Kira and I had gone from Isaac's to Clive's, it made sense that these were the steps within the network. How far reaching the web, or whose house was next, I hoped we'd never find out.

I lay my head on the pillow beside Kira trying not to let my imagination conjure images of what she'd been through. Kira stirred and moaned. Her eyelids flickered as she struggled to open them.

"Shsh," I whispered and laid my hand on her shoulder. "You're okay. You're eyes are swollen. I think your nose might be broken."

A tear slipped from the corner of her closed eye. I wiped it with my finger. I wanted to tell her who I was and that I was here to get her out. But I didn't want to make false promises. I also didn't want the others to hear me. It was too soon to judge their loyalty to Clive. From what I'd seen and heard so far I doubted these women had the same sense of duty and gratitude like those at Isaac's. But Stockholm Syndrome was unpredictable.

"You're okay," I said rubbing Kira's arm. I knew she wasn't, but what else could I say under the circumstances. I looked around the room for Julia. She was leaning against the wall in the far corner, dozing. "Is there something we can do?" I asked of anyone that might be listening. "Is there water down here? A cloth? Anything?"

A young girl, no more than fourteen, leaned up on her elbow. She shook her head. "They don't give us stuff like that."

"How do you wash yourself?"

"Clive takes us to the shower upstairs before we go to work." She lay back on her mattress.

"Fuck him," I said. Finding Kira had revived me. A way out was the next step.

I got up and headed for the stairs.

"What are you doing?" It was Julia's voice.

"I'm telling them I need some water and a cloth and some ice for…for her." I pointed to Kira, thanking God I'd caught myself before saying her name.

Julia laughed. "Are you crazy? You'll probably get beat up for that."

I laughed and pointed at my still bruised and swollen face. "I think I'm beyond that now. And we can't just leave her like this. If they want to make any money off her she needs some attention."

I climbed the stairs and knocked on the door. The girls below me collectively held their breath.

The door swung open. Clive had a look of surprise on his face. "What?"

"I need some water and ice to take care of the girl. She's no good to you looking like that. I'll clean her up."

"Who're you, Florence Nightingale?"

"She can't work like that. I'm just offering."

He scratched the back of his head and looked me up and down then glanced at the kitchen sink and back to me again. Settling his hands on his hips he studied the floor for a minute then slowly raised his head. "Okay, nursemaid." He walked to the sink and filled a bowl with water, lifted a dishrag from the counter and dropped it in then came back and handed it to me.

"Ice." I said, taking the bowl from him.

"Take what you get." He waved me away with his hand and closed the door behind me.

Descending the steps I was aware of my shaking hands and rubber knees, but in spite of that, I smiled. At the bottom

I looked around the room, six pairs of eyes met mine in disbelief. I made my way to Kira and promised that fear would not be my demise.

She dozed on and off as I cleaned the blood from her face as best I could. I remembered Eve saying 'don't rub' when I'd applied a warm towel to the welts on her back and I did the same now to Kira. Touching the cloth to her skin gently, dabbing, not wiping the blood away. She reached out and took my hand, not to stop me, just to hold it. I squeezed back, letting her know I understood.

The door opened and Clive came halfway down the stairway.

"Let's go," he said.

The girls immediately rose and walked to the stairs. I didn't move.

He nodded to Kira. "Is she awake?"

I shook my head. "Still unconscious," I lied. "She shouldn't be left alone. I'll stay with her. You probably don't need a dead whore on your hands."

He shrugged. "Wouldn't be the first time." He turned and went back up the stairs. "Let's go," he said again over his shoulder.

In procession, the girls mounted the stairs and the door closed behind them. The lock clicked into place.

Kira squeezed my hand. I lay down on the mattress beside her and rested my head close to hers. "There are things I need to tell you," I whispered. "The others are gone now, but when they're here we can't speak of any of what I'm about to say. Do you understand?"

Her eyes were still closed, but she nodded and turned her head toward me.

"My name is Britt. I'm a friend of your father's. I work as a private investigator. He got your postcard from *OK* and I went into Isaac's farm looking for you."

Tears ran from her eyes through her hair and into the mattress beneath her head. She gripped my hand in both of hers.

"I met Ruth. She told me that she taped the postcard back together and mailed it. She loved you."

Kira nodded and I thought I saw the hint of a smile on her cracked lips.

"Anyway, it was just the luck of the draw, if you can call it luck, that I was sold to Clive and now we're both here in Shangri-La. Some things are meant to be. Your father has never stopped looking even though the police did. They called you a runaway. Were you?" I asked her.

She started to shake her head, but winced. Her lips parted. "No," she whispered. "Well, yes, at first. I drifted from one friend's house to another. They hid me. Then I started going to the homeless shelters. I didn't go to school because I knew my father would find me. I wanted to make him suffer. I blamed him for my mother, my mother's…" She started to cry. "He had nothing to do with it. I know that now. He loved her. But I had to blame someone." She raised her hand to wipe tears from her cheek, but moaned and dropped it back to the mattress. "I was in the park. It was at least a year ago, but longer I think. I'm not sure. Isaac approached me. He said if I went with him for a couple of days I'd feel better. I missed my mom. I felt alone and still so angry. I wasn't ready to go home. I was stupid and selfish. I deserve this. I deserve what's happened to me."

"Don't cry," I said, dabbing away her tears with the cloth. "No one deserves this."

"There's no way to leave. If we try they'll kill us. You see how I look? Myles did this because I opened a window in the bedroom. He said someone could have seen me. I can't take the beatings anymore. I'll do what they say from now on. I want to live even if it means living like this."

"Forced sex and beatings are not my idea of living."

"You don't understand." She turned her head away from me. "But you will," she whispered.

I lay back and stared up at the ceiling listening to the steady breathing of her sleep, the best thing for her on many levels. She was so beautiful and too young to be harboring the demons she lived with. It had never occurred to me that Kira would be anything but overjoyed to see me and that together we'd plan our way out. Now, not only did I have to figure out how to escape. I had to convince her that it was worth the risk.

Tomorrow I'd play the guilt card and tell her how much her father needed her. How his life had fallen apart without her. It was my last ditch effort to give her the resolve she needed, but for now I had to work on my own. I closed my eyes and tried to remember the feel of Griff's hand holding mine. Denying the voice in my head that said I'm tainted goods and that he'd never want to hold my hand again.

SUNDAY

Beside me, Kira stirred as two of the girls crawled past us toward the bagels that had hit the floor at the bottom of the stairs. They tore into the bag like wild animals. Kira and I scrambled with the others, claimed our share of the slim offering and retreated to our lair, sinking our teeth into chewy dough.

"How're you feeling?"

"Better," she said. "You learn to heal pretty fast. If you don't, they have no use for you."

We took a few bites in silence.

"Does anyone else know?" she whispered.

I looked at her and raised my eyebrows, unsure of the question.

"Who you are. Why you're here?"

I shook my head. "We have to keep it that way."

"I don't know if I can do it."

"Escape?"

She nodded.

"You have to."

She looked across the room, her eyes somewhere beyond the filthy walls.

"You want to stay here forever?"

She looked at me, teary. "I'm scared."

"That makes two of us."

To pass the time I tried to talk with some of the women being held in the basement. A couple of them turned their heads away from me, fearful as trapped animals, which wasn't far from the truth. Marta had been a senior in high school and welcomed my questions. She seemed desperate for someone to care.

"My mother wouldn't answer me," she said. "I was screaming at her to make him stop."

"Him?"

"My uncle, her brother. She was alone with four kids. I'm the oldest. I told her I'd work. But my uncle said he would pay her right then. He waved a roll of bills in her face and said it was more than I could make at some low-level job. She took the money and closed the door. He put me in his car and brought me here."

Louise was mid-twenties, a prostitute that Clive had taken a liking to.

"Don't you ever think about escaping from this place?"

She looked at me and shook her head. "You're new. That's what everyone thinks about when they first get here. But sooner or later you give in."

She was quiet for a few minutes, twisting a strand of ratty hair around her finger. "I once watched Clive beat a girl to death for trying to leave. I was sitting in the van outside Rusty's. She tried to run into the woods, but he caught her."

"Are you sure he killed her?"

"He threw her body into the back of the van. Said he was taking her to the hospital after he dropped us off. I could see her eyes. They were open, but there was nothing there."

Julia had been in her second year at the university. These weren't lost souls like the women at Isaac's. These women had been taken from their lives, traded for money by boyfriends, uncles and hard as it was to believe, in Marta's case, her mother.

I went back to my mattress and lay down, pushing the images Louise's story had painted from my head. Kira and I were getting out. I would not succumb to fear. I'd been dozing off and on but came fully awake when Clive descended the stairs.

"You, you and you," he said pointing at Kira, Julia and me. "Shower, now." He jerked his thumb over his shoulder directing us to the floor above.

"We're going to the bar tonight," Kira said as we roused ourselves from our mattresses. "We always shower before we go."

"I wish we could shower after we go," Julia added climbing the stairs behind me.

The bar. I said the word over in my head imagining what that would entail. I thought about my initiation in the basement at Isaac's and my stomach turned over. I couldn't do it again. No stranger would grope my body. I'd cut his hands off first. I had to get out of here, tonight. I'd watch for a moment of opportunity at Rusty's. And when it appeared I'd grab it without a second thought. I'd have to keep Kira close at hand.

We walked down a hallway on the first floor of the house. Shades were drawn over the windows. The floor was gritty beneath my bare feet, salt and sand from the winter street outside. We took another flight of stairs and filed into a bathroom at the top of the landing.

"Hurry up," Clive said.

As I stepped past him, he handed me the pile of clothes he held in his hand. White jeans, a t-shirt and sneakers.

"Not quite in season," I said. But I was freezing, so anything was better than the mini skirt and sequined tank top I was still wearing from Isaac's.

Clive pushed me through the doorway, ignoring my comment.

Julia closed the door behind us. "I'll go first," she said and stripped down to her skin, dropping her clothes in a pile on the floor. She stepped into the shower and pulled the curtain.

I grabbed Kira's arm and turned her toward me. "Tonight," I whispered. "At the bar. We're getting out."

She shook her head. "There's no way. They watch every move. You'll see."

"No," I said, angry that I had to convince her. "You'll see. And when I say let's go, you better be ready."

"They'll kill us if they catch us. I've seen girls try. And I've never seen them again."

"Because they got away,"

"Because they caught them. They won't put up with us if we give them any shit. There's plenty more girls where we came from. Ones that obey."

Julia pulled back the curtain and stepped out. Kira stepped in and our conversation ended. When my turn came for the shower, I turned away from them as I undressed so they wouldn't see the red welts on my stomach. The scars on their bodies were from unthinkable acts of violence perpetrated by men they were forced to please. The ones on my stomach were self-inflicted.

Back in the basement we waited while the others showered.

"What time do we go?" I asked when all the women had had their turn upstairs..

Kira shrugged. "Whenever they feel like it."

"Are you okay?" Her eyes were still swollen. The blue beneath them was tinged with yellow. Her nose was puffy and red.

"What difference does it make?"

"I need you to be strong."

"I don't want to die."

"We're not gonna die. We'll make it. We have to."

She turned her head and looked at me. "I'd rather live like this than not live at all."

"Your father's falling apart. He's drinking. He's one step away from losing his job. He's been a mess since you disappeared. He has nothing. He needs you."

She looked at me and was about to answer when the lock at the top of the stairs clicked and the door swung open. "Let's go." It was Clive's voice.

Everyone stood and walked robotically to the stairs, ascending in single file.

The air was crisp and cold. I sucked it into my lungs, grateful to breathe something other than sweat, blood and the aftermath of sex. We climbed into a van, filling the three rows of bench seats. Myles slid into the passenger seat and Clive got behind the wheel. Myles wore a wool cap and when he turned to grin at all of us, his gold tooth glinted in the moonlight.

We drove through darkness, winding our way down a one-lane road. The headlights offered no details of our whereabouts, illuminating only pine trees lined up like sentries.

After twenty minutes or so lights broke through the blackness and a building took shape ahead of us. As we neared, I could make out the sign, *Rusty's*, and ten cars in the lot. The side of the van slid open and we stepped out one after the other. Clive and Myles each had a rifle hanging from a strap over their shoulders. They nodded us into the building. Inside there were two or three times as many men as cars in the lot. It would be a busy night if we were taking care of all of them. I needed an out fast.

We were claimed almost before we got all the way inside the bar. A young guy with a scar on his cheek and a knife in his belt took Kira by the arm and pulled her toward him. "What're you drinking?" he asked her.

I tried to follow, not wanting to lose sight of her, but felt myself being pulled in another direction. Turning, I saw a burly man in a red plaid jacket reeling me in. Yellow teeth appeared in crooked line between his mustache and beard. My stomach dropped. He handed me a shot glass and for the one and only time that night, I was grateful. He pulled me onto his lap after I sucked down the drink and groped my t-shirt. Several more shots were lined up on the table. I risked one more.

Above the bar there was a television playing the nightly news. The sound was turned down, but I almost leaped to my feet when Griff's face appeared with John beside him. I looked for Kira, but her back was to the bar. No one was paying attention. Across the bottom of the screen a ticker tape scrolled: *Prostitution ring busted in St. Bart, Maine.* Isaac's face appeared and the farmhouse loomed behind him. Then Chief Stebbins was on the screen. *Town official arrested,* the tape went on. I wondered how they got Stebbins. Had Isaac talked or was Stebbins still at the house when they raided it? Isaac was the tip of the iceberg in a prostitution ring, but hopefully they'd have figured that out. It would come to light as long as Isaac gave up his connections in Canada. But what if Isaac and Stebbins refused to talk and Griff and John had no idea where I was? What if Isaac didn't know what happened to the girls he sold to Lucas? What if Griff never realized that Kira and I had crossed the border? I could hope I was wrong, but hope wasn't going to get me out of here.

The guy beneath me finished his Budweiser, tossed back a shot and said, "Let's go." Shoving me off his lap, he took my elbow and led me to the men's room, inside the stench of urine made my eyes water. Booger, as I'd heard him called at the bar, unzipped his pants then reached for mine.

"Get the fuck away from me," I said.

He wrapped his hand around my neck and held me against the wall. "A feisty one," he laughed and slipped his other hand into the waistband of my jeans.

I brought up my knee fast and made contact with his thigh, missing my mark.

"Cut the shit, bitch," he said and landed a right hook against my stomach.

I vomited the two whiskeys I'd just downed onto his forearm. They dripped from the sleeve of his flannel shirt onto the floor.

"Jesus Christ," he said letting go of me and walking toward the sink.

I leaned against the wall for a minute to catch my breath. My vision was blurry from a lack of oxygen, whiskey or both, but I could still see the tiny window above the urinal and wondered if there was a similar one in the ladies room and if I could fit through. "I have to go to the bathroom," I said.

He nodded toward the urinal. "Go ahead."

"I want to go to the ladies room."

"Ladies." He scoffed at the word then nodded toward the door while he rinsed the vomit from his sleeve. "Get the fuck outta here. But don't think I'm done with you. You got a lesson comin' before the nights over. I'm gettin' my money's worth."

I slipped past him. Inside the ladies room Kira and a girl I didn't know were peeing. Stroke of luck, I thought. I stood on the toilet and checked the window. Locked of course.

"Are you really that stupid?" the girl asked. "You think they haven't thought of that? Even if it was unlocked Myles is outside patrolling." She laughed and disappeared out the door.

"I'm breaking this and we're getting out," I said to Kira.

"She's right. Someone will hear us."

"Not over the music. And Myles can't cover the whole building at once. This is our chance and we're taking it."

"We can't fit."

She was no more than a hundred and ten pounds and I wasn't much more than that. The window was about twelve inches high and eighteen wide. I took off my sneaker, slid my hand inside it and punched the window as hard as I could. Glass shattered and splintered around my arm. I pulled back through, a thin line of blood appeared on my forearm. I drove my shoe into the glass again, widening the opening. I glanced at Kira, she was pale and breathing in short gasps.

"Hurry," she said.

After punching out as much of the glass as I could, I slipped my shoe back on and stepped up onto the back of the toilet. I reached both arms through first then my head and shoulders. I reached for something to hold onto, but my hands kept coming up empty. Digging my elbows into the frozen ground I pulled myself through. Jagged glass on the edge of the window ripped through my t-shirt and into my stomach. Adrenaline drove me. I was almost all the way out tasting freedom when something solid connected with the side of my head and everything went black.

TUESDAY

I could hear the women's voices. Julia and Louise. I listened for Kira. They were speaking too softly, their words indiscernible. It was dark as pitch, not even a shadow. I felt the mattress beneath me and realized I was home and then cursed myself for calling it that. Something touched the side of my head. It was then I realized my eyes were closed. I turned. Mistake. Pain streaked through my skull, radiating into my neck and shoulders.

"Don't move." It was Julia's voice.

I tried to form a word, just one…Kira. I wanted to know if she was okay, but my mouth would not oblige.

"Shh," Julia said. "Don't talk."

Something touched my head again. This time I didn't move. It was cold. Ice wrapped in a cloth. The women's voices were slipping away. I gripped at the mattress trying to keep myself present, but the room fell from my grasp.

When I woke again it was quiet. This time my right eye cooperated and I could see the dim light shining in the corner of the basement. I turned my head toward it and rolled my body to follow immediately regretting the movement. Nausea enveloped me and I swallowed the acid in my mouth. For once I was glad I hadn't eaten. The room was empty. It must be night, the girls at work.

I went over the details that I could remember, but there wasn't much. The frozen ground, the shards of glass against my stomach and then nothing. I ran my palm beneath my shirt and felt the torn skin below my ribs. Something sharp was embedded above my hipbone. I winced as I pulled it free and held it up in front of my face. A piece of glass a half-inch long. I studied it considering its value as a weapon against them...or myself. I slipped it into the pocket of my jeans. I woke sometime later to the girls returning, their feet were heavy on the wooden stairs. I stirred and Julia knelt beside me peering into my face.

"You're awake?"

I started to nod, thought the better of it and whispered, "Yes."

"I wasn't sure you would still be with us," she said lying beside me. "Thought he might have killed you."

"Who?"

"Myles. The butt of his rifle, he almost drove it right through your head. I thought you were dead when he threw you into the van."

"Kira?"

"Sold."

The room closed in. I forced back the scream that rose in my throat and waited until I could breathe. "To who?"

She shrugged. "Who knows? He and Myles brought you both back here that night. Clive threw you down here and kept Kira upstairs. Haven't seen her since. That was two nights ago. You've been fading in and out."

"Did he kill her?"

"I doubt it. She was worth too much to kill. I'm sure he sold her."

I closed my eyes, too devastated to speak. I'd had her and I'd let her slip away. Now we were both missing, two of the millions of lost girls. I thought of Amy and hoped Griff hadn't told her anything. It would kill her to know what was going on. My big plan to be a hero had failed on all counts.

WEDNESDAY

The next morning when the bakery bag hit the floor I was able to open both of my eyes…progress. Julia handed me a bagel and I struggled into a sitting position. My head throbbed with every bite, but I hadn't eaten in days and hunger outweighed the pain of chewing. I'd just swallowed the last of it when the door at the top of the stairs opened and Clive came halfway down.

"You," he said pointing at me. "Come upstairs."

"Shit," Julia breathed beside me. "He's gonna make you pay."

I stood hunched over keeping one hand on my thigh for stability and worked my way over the mattresses and across the room to the stairs feeling like a sheep on its way to slaughter. Crawling up the stairs doggy style, I straightened at the top and followed Clive down the hall into a living room strewn with empty bottles and overflowing ashtrays. Myles sat in a chair with a bottle of Smirnoff's between his legs. He laughed when he looked at me. I hadn't seen my face since he'd hit me with the butt of his rifle and didn't want to. Before I'd made it to the center of the room, Clive planted his boot in my stomach, driving me back toward the doorway. I hit the wall and sank to the floor gasping.

"I told you, my girls don't leave." He lifted me by the front of my shirt twirled me around and shoved me backward into the room.

I fell in front of Myles who drove the pointed toe of his boot into my chest with enough force to lay me on my back. Clive leaned down and grabbed the neck of my shirt, pulling me to my feet. Once I was standing, he punched me in the stomach. Blood filled my mouth and I spit it onto his rug.

"Clean that up, you whore," he said and kicked my feet out from under me so I landed hard on my butt. Pain shot through my head. He knelt beside me, put his palm on the back of my skull and ground my face into the carpet where I'd spit the blood.

I vomited my bagel onto the rug. He rubbed my face in the mix. When he stopped I fell onto my side and curled into a fetal position.

A towel landed on the floor beside me. "Wipe up the mess you made," he said.

I reached out with one hand and rubbed the towel in the vomit. Smearing it over the rug.

"Jesus. You're worthless. Get up." He wrapped his hand around my upper arm and pulled me to standing then shoved me toward the hallway and back to the door that led to the basement.

As he turned the knob, I lifted my hand and raised one finger asking him to stop a moment.

He laughed. "You want to speak? Go ahead, if you can."

I looked at him and he waited. I pulled together any strength I had left to form the words. "Why didn't you kill me?"

He smiled and leaned close to my face. "Because you're gonna make me some money first." Then he lifted his boot placed it against my stomach and sent me somersaulting down the steps.

When I hit the bottom I didn't move. I couldn't. I stayed there curled in a ball feeling lucky. I used to think luck meant hitting the lottery or avoiding the flu. Now luck meant, not raped, not dead.

I maneuvered myself into a sitting position, propped up by the basement wall. The others looked at me. Julia started to get up, but I raised my hand to stop her. Sitting here was as much as I could do at least for a while.

I let my hand fall to the floor beside me. It landed on something scratchy. I took it in my fingers and lifted the thing to see what it was. A bag, the bakery bag, empty of course, but across it in blue letters, *Campbell's* and beneath it, *Grand Falls, New Brunswick*. Why hadn't I thought to look at it before? Or had it not been there? Had Clive switched shops? It didn't matter. None of it mattered. It was there now. Tears came to my eyes. I knew where I was. Now I just needed a way to tell Griff.

SUNDAY

Three days passed without Clive pointing at me to shower and get ready for work. But by the fourth day the side of my head had decreased in size according to Julia, and my face looked almost normal except for the yellow and purple skin beneath my eyes. My head still throbbed and my vision was blurry in my right eye, the remnants of a concussion, no doubt. But I could breathe again. The cuts on my stomach from the shattered window were healing and I still had the sliver of glass in my pocket should I feel the need to add new ones. Just knowing I had the ability to do so was comfort enough.

Clive descended the stairway and this time, after singling out Louise and Julia, he pointed to me. "Shower time," he said. When we reached the door to the bathroom he nodded to the shirt I was wearing, a shredded mess of blood and vomit. "Give me that," he said.

I hesitated.

"Now."

I slipped it off and let it drop to the floor.

He kicked my filthy t-shirt into the corner of the hallway, handed me the bag he'd been carrying and nodded me into the bathroom. "Hurry up," he said, then lit a cigarette and sat in the wooden chair outside the door.

When Louise was finished Julia looked at me. "Go ahead," she said.

I stepped into the shower stall and closed my eyes reveling in the sensation. Water rained down on my skin, cleansing the stench of dried blood and erasing the fingerprints of my trespassers. The curtain pushed aside and

Julia stepped in behind me. She didn't speak. She rubbed soap on a cloth and washed my back and then my hair. I hadn't felt kindness in so long that it crushed my guard. I fell against her and let her hold me. Neither of us spoke.

"Hurry up," Clive pounded his fist against the door.

We dried and dressed quickly. My new blouse was a pink and blue floral design with buttons down the front and sheer enough that I longed for something, anything to put beneath it. We followed Clive back to the basement and waited while the others showered. Then we drove the same route we had the last time I'd been in the van, a long twisting stretch through darkness. The leaf less limbs of the trees reached across the road like arthritic fingers. Myles was again in the passenger seat, a rifle across his knees. He laughed when I stepped inside the van.

"Gonna behave this time?" he asked.

I'm not the religious type. I never even talked to God as a kid. Not even on those nights when Amy and I were alone. I figured if God knew everything then He sure as hell knew what Amy and I were dealing with and He should have stepped in and done something without waiting for an eight year old to ask. So why I was praying now, inside this van and why I thought He'd hear me now if He hadn't then, I wasn't sure. But I couldn't handle another set of hands on me or another dick with a dick. I was losing clarity of the fact that I was on a job and I was not one of these girls.

When we pulled into Rusty's a dozen or more cars were in the lot. I hoped Booger wouldn't be there. I hoped nobody would find me attractive. My face still advertised the leftovers of a beating. I told myself that no one would want me so I could convince my legs to hold me up as I walked from the van to the building. Inside, I slipped away from the others as they walked to the middle of the room for the men to appraise them. I sidled up to an empty stool at the edge of the bar and hoped to blend in. The bartender noticed, but didn't say anything instead he poured Jack Daniels three fingers high into a dirty glass and set it in front of me. At first I thought he was being kind, but then he leaned in close and his stale beer breath hit my face. "I'll take a break soon and you and me are goin' out back."

I swallowed the JD in two gulps. He filled my glass again and winked. "You ain't no cheap date," he said.

Two men bellied up at the other end of the bar. "Hey Rusty," one of them yelled. "I'm thirsty. Get you tired, old ass down here."

Rusty cackled and winked again. "Don't you go nowhere, sweetheart, old Rusty's gonna take care of you and visy-versy." He cackled again and moved toward the two men.

In front of me on the bar was a small, yellow pencil, the kind they give you when you play miniature golf. Rusty was still at the other end, shooting the shit with the two draft beer guys. I reached for the pencil, my heart beating a hole in my chest and waited for Myles or Clive to grab me from behind. I wrapped my hand around the pencil, slid it back to me and into my pocket. Nothing. I exhaled.

The door beside me swung open and I jumped. Two uniformed police stepped inside and surveyed the room. I almost started to cry. We were saved. I was just about to slide off my stool when Rusty was back in front of me. "Well, well, well, Officer Jarvais, where the hell you been?"

The cop stepped up beside me. He was fortyish and needed a shave. The veins in his nose said he liked to drink. "Enjoying yourself this evening?" he asked me.

I nodded. His breath smelled like ham and cheese.

"Give me what she's having," he said and tipped his head toward my glass.

Julia appeared on my right. "Michael," she said.

His eyes lit up. "Julia, I didn't see you when I came in."

He took his drink from the bar then Julia's elbow and together they walked toward the darkened hallway that led to the bathrooms.

I looked for the other cop and saw that he hadn't moved from his stance just inside the door. He was young, so young he looked more like a kid on Halloween wearing his dad's uniform than a real cop. I pegged him for a rookie just out of the academy, clean-shaven, fair complexion, scared and uncomfortable. *Maybe*...I thought.

"I got an empty seat," I called to him.

He looked my way. "No thank you ma'am. I'm fine right here."

They had to be on the take, at least Jarvais was, that much was obvious and this kid was getting his initiation into life as a small town cop. Free booze and sex and in return the cops looked the other way when it came to doing business at Rusty's. Or they partook in it like Jarvais. This kid was learning the ropes and not too happy about it from the look on his face.

I slid off my stool and walked up close to him. I had to take a chance. "Please," I whispered, running my hand over his crotch to make it look good to anyone who might be watching. "I don't want anything. I need help." I took him by the hand and pulled him toward the bar. "C'mon, what's one drink?"

He followed me, his confusion obvious.

"What's your name kid?" Rusty asked.

"Marshall," he said. "Officer Marshall."

"Well then, Officer Marshall, what'll it be?" Rusty set a small, white cocktail napkin in front of the cop and my mouth dropped open. There it was again...luck.

"Just a Coke," he said.

Rusty laughed. "Ain't nobody drinkin' just a Coke in my establishment. He filled a glass half full with Coke and topped it off with Myer's Rum then set it in front of the kid and moved away to another customer.

I put my hand on Officer Marshall's thigh.

"Don't," he said.

I nuzzled his neck. "I'm going to give you a number and you better call it. And you better not say a fucking word to anyone, not your partner, not anyone. I'm not one of them."

He looked at me, confused and lifted his drink pretending to take a sip.

I slipped the napkin into my lap and glanced down the bar for Rusty. He was at the other end filling glasses. Behind him, in the mirror I could see Clive. He was sitting with his profile to me and I prayed one more time that he wouldn't look my way. I slipped the pencil from my pocket, wrote Griff's cell number on it and *Rusty's Bar, Grand Falls, New Brunswick*. Then I crumpled it into my palm and shoved my hand into the cop's crotch. When he reached to stop me, I slipped the napkin into his hand. Our eyes met and for the first time I could see that he understood. I leaned into his neck again. "Please," I whispered.

"Put your dick back in your pants, Marshall," Jarvais said coming up beside us. "Time to go."

Officer Marshall stood and like a new puppy, followed Jarvais to the door. Just before stepping outside he turned back, looked at me and nodded.

"Looks like he likes you," Rusty said refilling my glass. "Now I'm gonna see if I like you too." He came around the bar picked up my glass in one hand and with the other pulled me roughly off the stool and toward the swinging kitchen door.

I walked behind him beneath pans hanging overhead and remembered the same image in Isaac's kitchen. How long had I been doing this? Like the other girls, my sense of time was nonexistent. He opened a door in the back corner of the kitchen and we stepped into a makeshift bedroom. A cot stretched along one wall covered with a grimy sheet and stains that said I wasn't the first girl back here. He sat me on the bed, stood in front of me and unzipped his pants. His penis flopped out, flaccid and wrinkled.

I looked away, the lump in my throat growing bigger and more painful.

"Suck it," Rusty said. He wrapped his hand around the back of my head and pressed my face into his groin.

I didn't move. He pulled my head back with his right hand and backhanded me with his left. His ring opened my cheek.

"Hurry up. I ain't got all night. I already gave ya two drinks you ungrateful bitch." His left fist caught my cheek smearing blood over my lips.

I opened my mouth and gagged as he shoved himself inside. I considered biting down as hard as I could but knew it would only mean another beating and so I performed and I tried not to admit that I'd given in. My eyes watered. I thought I would vomit as he slammed himself against my face. I gagged again, pulled away from him and spit onto the floor. He stepped back, adjusted his pants and wrestled with his zipper.

"Here," he tossed me a cloth. "I gotta get back to work." He walked out and closed the door.

I lifted the cloth to my mouth and vomited into it then rolled it in a ball and threw it under the bed. I sat on the edge of the filthy mattress and told myself I'd done what I had to. A blowjob didn't make me one of them, but I knew now why they did it. Survival. And again, I told myself that I was lucky. He hadn't put his hands on my skin or shoved himself between my legs. And then I started to cry. Griff would never want me again. I shook my head, driving out that reality and telling myself I was wrong. I couldn't admit to it yet, because the thought of seeing Griff was the only thing holding me together.

The door opened. Myles stood with his rifle pointing at me. All I could think of was that Officer Marshall had told them about the note and now I was going to die. I won't save Kira or see Amy or Griff again. A wave of sadness hit me, but with it came profound relief. It was over.

"Time to go," he said. "Get your ass outside."

I reached for my drink on the bedside table, swallowed it down and followed him out the door.

SUNDAY

By my count, which wasn't exact by any stretch, it had been about two weeks since I'd slipped the napkin with Griff's number on it to the young cop at Rusty's. And every night when we went back to the bar I told myself that tonight Griff would walk in the door. Tonight I would be saved, but hope was slipping away and acceptance taking over. Officer Marshall's allegiance was to the police department certainly not to some whore in a rundown bar in the middle of nowhere. He'd probably thrown the napkin away as soon as he'd left the building.

Every day was the same. Wake up, eat a bagel and lie on our filthy mattresses until Clive or Myles came to collect us for showers. My teeth had begun to ache from a lack of calcium, my body was no longer my own and nothing I wanted to claim. I detached myself from it and gave it over to the hands and mouths, the fingers and tongues of the men at Rusty's. I hated every inch of my skin and defiled it every chance I got. I became obsessed with the piece of glass I'd saved from my attempted escape. At night, when we'd return from Rusty's I'd slide it over my stomach eager for the physical pain, eager to punish myself for what I'd become. When I thought about Griff and Amy the grief was unbearable. I thought instead about the girls at Isaac's, ashamed of my naïveté toward them. I'd been incredulous that they would call themselves lucky when all they got was a beating and in my ignorance, I'd wondered how they'd ever gotten to that point. Now I too was grateful for black and blue skin instead of a penis thrust in my face or between my legs.

The night was not as frigid as most and I wondered as I sat in the van beside Julia if we were in the annual January thaw and when exactly had Christmas come and gone? We rattled over potholed, muddy roads and finally pulled into Rusty's familiar parking lot. I used to count the cars parked and estimate the number of men inside, but I didn't anymore. What difference did it make?

We filed inside. Booger was at the table to my right and smiled. I walked past him not making eye contact. Big George was just beyond him. George preferred using his belt and so did I. I walked over and pulled out the chair across from him.

"Can I sit down?" I asked.

He smiled and nodded. "Stay there," he said. "I need a drink."

"Get me something too," I called after him.

I was halfway turned in my chair watching George collect our drinks when the door opened and Griff walked in. John was behind him and an army of cops followed. I wasn't sure I was seeing right. I was afraid to move. Afraid that if I jumped up and ran to him he wouldn't be real and when I reached to touch him I'd wake up on a mattress in Clive's basement. Worse, I was afraid he wouldn't recognize me. I was so thin and filthy and bruised. I sat frozen to my chair.

Clive ran for the hallway near the bathrooms, men on his heels. A shot was fired and everything came to a dead stop. Nobody moved for a second or two and then it started again. Chaos. I still couldn't move, but the knowledge that it was real was sinking in. And then Griff looked at me. Our eyes held and he came toward me. He knelt in front of me and took my face between his hands and pulled me to him, our foreheads touching, our cheeks wet with each other's tears and finally his lips on mine. I dissolved against him. He was real.

I looked up from his shoulder to see police snapping handcuffs on the men around us. John had corralled the girls into one corner and was desperately searching their faces.

I looked at Griff and shook my head. "She's not here," I said. "But she was."

"John," Griff yelled over the noise. "John," he called again.

Detective Stark made his way to us. "Jesus, Britt," was all he said when he looked at me. There were tears in his eyes.

"She was here," I said. "We tried to escape, together. We got caught. They sold her. I don't know where she is." I started to cry. "I'm so sorry, John, I said. "I'm so sorry…"

I felt John's hand on mine. He pulled up to standing and wrapped me in his arms. "Britt," he said. "You've done more than you ever should have. I'm the one who's sorry. Let's get you out of here."

Across the room the girls were seated at a table. An officer was taking down their information. Julia caught my eye and smiled. I smiled back at her as I slipped out of John's embrace and into Griff's. Together, we walked out of Rusty's.

A fleet of police cars their lights flashing, were parked in a horseshoe around the front door. I saw Clive in the backseat of a cruiser. He watched me walk past with Griff. I wondered what was going through his head.

"How'd you know?" I asked, hoping Officer Marshall had found the balls he needed.

"A cop called me this morning, young guy, new on the force. Said a woman at Rusty's gave him my number."

"Officer Marshall."

"Yup."

"Took him long enough to grow a pair," I said. "And now they'll kill him."

"He's being transferred and more than happy to go."

We stopped outside of John's black Suburban. I leaned against the door and looked up at Griff. Every time I looked at him I started to cry partly out of disbelief that he was really here and partly because I was already feeling a sense of loss. How could he stay with me after all that had happened? At Isaac's I'd planned to lie to him. Lie by omission and keep what had happened to myself, but I knew that was impossible now. He'd walked into Rusty's, he knew what was going on, knew that I was just another whore and had been for weeks.

"Griff," I said, the words that were forming already breaking my heart. "It's okay. You don't...I mean I understand. So much...I tried not to...but I...they wouldn't..."

He put his fingers beneath my chin and raised my face to his. "I love you," he said. "I never should have let you do this. Whatever happened is over. It's all over. We're together." He pulled me against him and buried his face in my hair. "I thought I'd never find you." His voice cracked. He opened the back door of the Suburban. "Get in. There are enough cops here to handle this. They don't need me."

I sniffed back my own tears, wiped my cheeks and was suddenly painfully aware of how I looked. My sheer blouse, wild uncombed hair, bruised body. "I'm sorry, I..." I looked down at myself. "I'm filthy and dirty and, and..."

He put his arm around my shoulders and kissed my forehead. "When I walked into that bar and saw you sitting there, no one has ever looked more beautiful."

He took a grey wool blanket from the back of the Suburban and wrapped it around me. I leaned against him and we sat in the quiet and watched the arrests being made and the girls being loaded into a police van, taking their first step toward home. Beneath my ear, Griff's heart pounded in his chest.

John opened the front door and climbed in. Revving the engine, he turned to me. "I know there's a lot to discuss, but you need rest before we start. He looked me up and down.

"Looks like you need this too." He tossed a gray sweatshirt that read CID into my lap from the front seat.

I smiled and pulled it over my head. "Thanks, John," I said.

"But you did see her?" he asked.

"More than saw her. We were together for…I'm not sure, but maybe a week or more. She'd been at Isaac's and was sold to Clive. That's where I found her."

"Is she," his voice broke and he cleared his throat. "She's okay?"

"She's strong and careful. She wants to get home. That's why Isaac sold her. She kept trying to escape." In the rearview mirror I could see the hint of a smile on John's face, the proud father. "She feels terrible about what she's done and what she's put you through. She loves you."

He nodded, sniffed and wiped his eye with the back of his hand. "You sure as hell look like you need a good meal. I don't know what's open this time of night, but we'll find something." He put the car in drive.

"Just no bagels," I said and settled in against Griff. Something sharp dug against my thigh. I reached into my pocket and pulled out the shard of glass I'd held onto for so long. Leaning toward the door, I pressed the button, lowered the window and tossed it into Rusty's parking lot.

FINDING KIRA
MONDAY

John offered a stop at the nearest ER, but I declined. After a plate of bacon, eggs and waffles, he drove the six hours back to Portland. I knew he was champing at the bit for information, but he kept his questions broad and I was grateful. John's an experienced interrogator and it didn't take a genius to see that I was barely holding it together. The details would come soon enough.

The first thing I'd asked for once my stomach was full, was a shower. The second thing was sleep. At Griff's apartment under a hot spray of water and camouflaged by steam, I braved an inventory of cuts and bruises.

"You okay?" Griff called through the door. "Need any help?"

"I'm okay," I answered.

There was nothing I wanted more than to feel Griff's skin on mine, but that would have to wait until I could hide myself from his full view beneath a blanket or in a darkened bedroom. But it was morning now and the sun was streaming through the window. He'd cringed at the yellowish, blue skin beneath my eyes, remnants of Clive's fist. There was no way I could let him see the extent of violence on my body, some of it by my own hand. I walked into the bedroom with his terrycloth bath sheet wrapped around me, but it wasn't big enough to hide the toe print Myles' boot had left on my chest.

Griff was sitting on the bed and started to get up when he saw the bruise. "Jesus."

I held up my hand. "Don't say anything, please. I can't talk about it now. But I will. Just let me sleep first. Tell John to come over this afternoon."

Griff nodded and moved toward the door.

"And Griff," I touched his arm as he passed. "Will you call Amy?"

"Of course," he said and closed the door behind him.

I lay between the sheets relishing the sensation of soft cotton on clean skin. I wanted more than anything to have Griff here beside me, to tell him every detail of my time away from him, but I was so afraid of the outcome that I was postponing the conversation. Once he knew the truth of how my body had been violated I'd be repulsive to him and our life together would be over. He'd said I was wrong about that, but the adrenalin high we were both running on now would wear off and when it did reality would set in. Then again, if I didn't tell him the truth right up front, he'd imagine the worst and he'd be right.

He was rustling around in the kitchen. I slipped out of bed and walked naked across the plush, bedroom carpet, took a deep breath and opened the door. He must have heard me because before I made it down the hallway, he appeared. I stood before him with all my wounds in full view, even those I had created myself. He didn't speak, nor did I. He approached me, keeping his eyes on my body, not my face. I turned my back to him, disclosing in full detail my time with Isaac and Clive as well as the ribbons of scars from Edward. When he was close enough to touch me he raised his eyes and looked at my face. His cheeks were wet.

"I'm a mess," I said. "And the inside's worse. I'm not going kid myself into thinking I'm still desirable to you. So let's part as friends. You don't have to love me." And with that I lost it. I covered my face with my hands and my body convulsed with grief.

He laid his hands on my shoulders and pulled me against him. "Forgive me," he said. "I never should have let you go in there. Of course I love you. Nothing could make me leave you, especially not this.

"But I've done things...I couldn't...I tried not to, but...Griff, I'm the one that needs forgiveness."

He took a step back and looked at me. "Britt, whatever happened, whatever you did, you did to survive. If you hadn't, you wouldn't be standing here. What you did kept you safe until you could find a way out, until you could hand off that note. What you did got you out."

He wrapped his arms around me and held me tight against him. We stood in silence, holding on, crying into each other's shoulders and then he led me to bed. He tucked me in and then went to the other side, stripped down and got in beside me. I pasted myself against him wanting to feel every inch of his skin on mine. His hands washed over me cleansing away the brutality. His touch was salve to my wounds and would heal me one layer at a time.

When I woke up Griff was gone. I lay still listening to voices coming from the kitchen. It was Griff speaking and then I heard John. I tossed back the covers. I'd made him wait long enough. From the bottom drawer of Griff's dresser I gathered the stash I kept there, a sweatshirt, tee shirt and pair of jeans.

They both looked up as I walked into the room. I pulled out a kitchen chair and joined them at the table. "Okay," I said. "I'm ready."

I took them through my days at Isaac's. I told them about Ruth and that she'd been the one to mail Kira's postcard. John said she'd told him the same thing when they'd picked her up along with Isaac. And it was Ruth who'd told them everything about Oracles of the Kingdom and had given them Stebbins.

"Where is she now?" I asked.

"At the women's correction center in Windham. She'll stay there until the trial, but she's been forthcoming about everything that went on at the farm. She'll get a deal."

Isaac and Stebbins were in the Fort Kent jail being held without bail until their trial dates. According to John, Rose had also been somewhat helpful, but still held an allegiance to Isaac. Isaac and Stebbins weren't talking, at least not yet.

Things got vague after leaving Isaac's. No doubt Lucas had connections at the border since I'd crossed without papers. I had no address for Clive's. I only knew that the house had to be near Campbell's Bakery, but I told them I thought I would recognize it. I still had the picture in my head of those basement steps and the locked front door that Lucas had taken me through. Ruth had told them about Lucas. As the middleman, he had most likely transported Kira again after Clive sold her. All hope was riding on Lucas, if we could find him and if he would talk.

"Even though Lucas doesn't live at the house, there's got to be information inside that will help us find him."

"The Grand Falls police are working on it and they may have notified the Canadian Security Intelligence Service since women were taken over the border. There's no street address in Clive's name so it's taking time to locate the place." John said. "I asked Chief LeBlanc to let me know as soon as they have something. Needless to say, Clive isn't talking."

"What about the girls?"

"Scared of repercussions if they say anything."

"Can't say I blame them."

"We're heading back up there in the morning," John said.

"I'll need to go to my apartment to get a few things." I glanced at Griff.

Griff leaned forward on the couch, his elbows on his thighs and looked at me. "This case now belongs to the Fort Kent and Grand Falls. Most likely the feds have been called too because of the border crossings. John and I are going back up to offer our assistance because Kira is still somewhere in the midst of it. But there's no 'you' in 'we'."

"You can't just bump me out." Tears stung my eyes. I blinked them back damned if I was going to cry. "I've invested more than either one of you in this case. I'm not walking away. I'm in it until we find Kira. I told her I'd get her out and that's not a promise I'm going to break."

Griff sighed and leaned back on the couch, his eyes on John. John pursed his lips and nodded and Griff looked back to me. "If, and that's a big if, you continue to work with us on this, under no circumstances will you do anything on your own. We're secondary to the Canadian police. They're allowing our involvement because of Kira. That means you're with me or with John at all times. No heroics. Got it?"

"Got it." In truth, even the thought of working alongside them scared me to death and imagining a confrontation with Lucas made it hard to breathe. But I couldn't tell Griff or John that. I knew too well what Kira was going through and that left me no choice.

There was a soft knock at the door and Griff went to answer it. A woman, her voice so soft...a familiar laugh. It was Amy. I jumped out of the chair and ran down the hall into Amy's anxious arms. We laughed and cried and hugged each other and then sat down still holding hands as though I would somehow disappear again if we let go. She touched the bruises on my face and demanded an explanation. I kept it vague, assuring her that they were nothing and I was fine. Lying through my teeth.

Griff worked around us setting the table. In the center, he placed a large bowl of his infamous spaghetti with Bolognese sauce. We took our seats and he kissed the top of my head as he reached past me to fill my plate. I blinked back tears. Less than twenty-four hours ago, I'd been sitting at Rusty's hoping to get beat up instead of raped.

After serving, Griff took the seat on my left, at the head of the table and made a toast. "To courage, perseverance and forgiveness," he said, his voice catching at the end.

We touched glasses all around, our Pinot Noir resting on John's Diet Coke. I swallowed the wine against a lump in my throat.

After dinner, I cleared the table and Amy washed the dishes. We chitchatted about things in her life and avoided mine. She didn't ask about the case we were working. She knew enough not to ask for answers she didn't want to hear. And I'd covered as much of my body as I could so she wouldn't have reason. At nine o'clock I closed the door behind her and John. I promised Amy that I'd call her first thing in the morning, but left out the fact that when I did call it would be from the road as we headed back to Canada.

Griff and I settled on the couch with a pint of Ben and Jerry's. We'd done this hundreds of times, but never had I considered myself lucky or fortunate. I'd been oblivious to the world while Chunky Monkey melted over my tongue. I dropped the spoon in the half-full bowl and set it on the table.

"Done already?" Griff asked.

"Guilty."

"What do you mean?"

"How can I sit here and eat ice cream while girls are abducted and sold for sex?"

Griff set his bowl beside mine. "It's a huge problem. What we're seeing is a drop in the bucket."

"These girls are existing on bagels. Alcohol and drugs are the only relief they have. I can't stop thinking about Kira and Julia and the rest of them. I feel like a deserter."

"The girls you were with are safe. *Oracles of the Kingdom* is defunct. Rusty's is closed. All that's because of you. When we find Kira, that'll also be because of you. You're no deserter."

"There's one other thing."

"What's that?"

"As much as I want to find Kira, I'm scared shitless at the thought of seeing Lucas again."

Griff nodded. "That's why we're making a stop before we meet John in the morning."

"Where?"

"McCreaty's Gun Shop and then the shooting range for a little practice. I want you to be able to protect yourself. Not saying you'll need to, but better safe than sorry."

TUESDAY

McCreaty's opened at seven-thirty and Griff and I were not alone standing outside the door waiting for the deadbolt to slide back. Who the hell needs a gun at seven-thirty in the morning? We had to meet John at the precinct at nine, so I understood our press for time. But the two guys waiting with us, shifting from foot to foot outside the door didn't look like they had any place to be other than somewhere sleeping it off.

Red McCreaty released the deadbolt promptly at seven-thirty and swung the door wide. The smile on his face widened seeing green on his doorstep at such an early hour. "Mornin' folks, come on in." He took a step back. The two men who had waited with us stepped past him and headed toward rifles standing vertically in a rack along the far wall. "What can I do you for?" he asked Griff.

"Need something lightweight, compact and comfortable for my friend." Griff nodded to me.

Red turned and we followed him. I made a face at Griff. *Friend?*

He shrugged at me behind Red's back. His look said, get over it.

Red led us to a glass case, inside were fifteen or twenty pistols, lots of options for ending someone's life. That's how I saw it. I wasn't much for weapons.

"What's it gonna be used for?" Red asked.

"Protection," Griff told him.

The thought of having to pull one of these out and aim it toward Lucas brought a mix of anticipation and anxiety. On one hand, I'd like nothing more than an opportunity for payback. On the other, I was afraid of Lucas so there was a chance, put in the situation, I'd fold.

"Griff," I tugged on his jacket. "I don't know if I can...this might be a waste of money."

He blew me off and turned back to Red.

"This little beauty is made for a woman," Red said. "It's a Charter Arms Pink Lady .38 Special Undercover Lite. She weighs just 12 ounces. Fits anywhere." He looked at me and winked.

I turned my back to him and scouted the store for the two men. One was holding a rifle peering through the sight. The other was beside him hunched over a glass case.

"What do you think?" Griff asked.

I shrugged. Buying a gun made me feel like something was going to happen. If I had a gun, I was going to use it. "It's okay," I said.

"Hold it. See how it feels." Red held the revolver in the palm of his hand.

I picked it up. "Light," I said. I wrapped my fingers around the grip. It fit perfectly, even felt comfortable. "It'll do." I handed it back to Red.

"Now I just need to see your permit."

Griff pulled the paperwork from his wallet and handed it to Red. I'd applied for the permit after deciding to join Griff's PI firm, but I'd never taken the next step and bought a gun. I liked the investigative end of the business and most of the time our cases called for more brains than brawn, but the players in this game were of a different breed.

Red glanced at the permit and handed it back. "How much ammo you need?"

"Couple boxes," Griff said. "We're heading to the range for some practice."

In less than ten minutes we were back in the car, Griff with his smug smile and me with my new Pink Lady.

"Look, I understand this makes you uncomfortable, but it gives me a little peace of mind. Nothing says you'll have to use it, but if you need to you'll have it."

"I know. I get it. But I'm not sure that I'll be able to use it even if I am in that kind of situation."

"You will," Griff said.

We drove toward the Falmouth Gun Club in silence. I thought about bending over the washing machine for Isaac and wondered how differently things might have gone if I'd had a gun on me. Isaac never would have raped me because I would have blown his fucking face off first. Maybe Griff was right. It was a good thing to have, just in case.

At the gun club, we walked past a row of shooters practicing from separate cubicles. Hanging the standard twenty-five yards in front of them was the silhouette of a man, each seeing a different face as they pulled the trigger. I had a collection of faces to imagine on mine.

Griff and I stepped inside an empty box and put on our protective gear then he handed me my shiny Pink Lady.

"It's a little cliché," I said looking at the girly gun.

He laughed. "Gotta have a sense of humor."

"Yeah, this is a real hoot."

After he'd loaded it, I took the gun from his hand and pointed it at the silhouette. Isaac loomed twenty-five yards out. Griff stood behind me and with his right hand at my elbow, raised my arm and steadied it with his own.

"Breathe," he said. "This is just practice. When you feel ready, pull the trigger."

I took a breath, clenched my teeth and squeezed. The recoil sent me backward into Griff's chest. When I looked at the shadow image in front of me, it was clean. Not a mark on it. "I think I shut my eyes," I said.

"That's okay. That's why we're practicing. Try it again. It's not so hard. Just aim and shoot."

I tried and retried and Griff loaded and reloaded and by my tenth shot I was keeping my feet solidly planted and my eyes open. I had yet to make a mark on Isaac's shadow, but I was getting comfortable. The Pink Lady and I were becoming friends. One more reload and Isaac's chest had sprouted three holes, his face was still unmarred, but I was getting closer.

"Chances are if you are shooting, it's not going to be from this distance. You'll be closer and more accurate."

"Is that supposed to make me feel better?"

"Just sayin'." He checked his watch. "We better go. John's eager to be on the road. He's gonna be a wreck until this is over."

"He's not alone," I said.

At the Portland Police Station, John was standing beside his black Suburban when we pulled up. "Where the hell you been?" He asked, leaning into the passenger window.

"Had an errand to do," Griff said, "McCreaty's." He nodded toward me.

John tapped his palm against the window frame. "Good idea. Park this thing in the back lot." He stepped away from the car. "And hurry the hell up."

Griff slipped his SUV into a space behind the building and we gathered our bags from the back. My new purchase was in a case, inside my bag. I could feel the hard edge of the box rubbing against my thigh with each step. Part of me was scared shitless to own a gun because of what I might do with it and part of me felt like an Amazon woman because I owned a gun and what I might do with it.

How's the department feel about this?" I asked John as he eased the Suburban onto Interstate 95 and headed north.

"They had Kira pegged as a runaway from the get-go. I never believed that. It's taken me three years to find her without their help. They feel like schmucks. And they should. I'm on leave for as long as I need to be."

"As usual, they did the least they could do," Griff said.

"I booked two rooms at a motel in Saint-Leonard," John said changing the subject. "It's no five star hotel, but you'll have a place to sleep."

"It'll do," Griff said. "That's all we'll need."

"First stop is Fort Kent. See if Stebbins or Isaac has decided to take a deal."

"What's the offer?" I asked.

"Either of them gives us Lucas, they get special consideration at sentencing."

"How special?" I asked pissed off that an offer was extended. They should get everything they had coming and then some, but I knew John would sell his soul to find Kira so I kept my mouth shut. This was his gig.

"I don't know. That's up to the judge and the district attorney."

Five hours and one pit stop later, John turned off the engine and we stepped out of the Suburban and into the police department's parking lot in Fort Kent, the northern most town in Maine.

We stopped in front of the desk sergeant who was on the phone debating a grocery list with...his wife? Girlfriend? Significant other?

"I don't like turkey bacon," he said. (Which was obvious by the jellyroll of flesh hanging over his belt.) Get the real deal or don't get anything." He held up a finger requesting us to wait until he got this matter settled with whoever was on the other end. "Yeah, yeah, 2% is okay. I can live with it. And Budweiser." He hung up the phone. "What can I do you for, folks?"

"Who's in charge of the investigation regarding Chief Stebbins and Isaac Bennett?" John asked.

"And you are?"

"Detective Stark," said a voice behind us.

We turned as a handsome, fiftyish man approached. He glanced disapprovingly at the officer behind the desk and extended his hand to John. "Detective Merridan. Come this way."

We followed him through an empty squad room, a half full box of donuts sat on a table next to a Mr. Coffee. A sticker on the front of one desk said "I'd rather be fishing."

Inside a corner office, Merridan closed the door. "I'm sorry to say that I haven't had much luck so far. We've emptied the *Oracles of the Kingdom* farm. Whole place is cordoned off in yellow tape and we're combing every inch. The women have been relocated to their families, friends or whatever we could do for them."

"Ruth's in Windham Prison?" I asked.

"Yes", Merridan said. "Isaac Bennett's daughter was taken to the women's facility."

"She's not a bad person."

"Tell it to the judge," he said.

"And Stebbins and Isaac?" Griff asked.

"They're downstairs. They'll stay until their arraignment."

"You get anything from them?"

"Zip. Neither one's talking."

"I don't want to step on any toes," John said. "But Bennett had my daughter for close to a year and she's still missing. Would you be willing to let me talk to him?"

Merridan hesitated. "I doubt you'll get anything."

"I'd like to try."

"Can't hurt, I suppose."

We followed Merridan down two flights of green metal stairs. He lifted a latch on a barred door. The hinges groaned open and we stepped into the holding area. A young cop looked up from the copy of *Hunter's Monthly* in his hand.

Merridan motioned John into a two by four room. He took a seat at the table. Griff and I went into an adjacent room to watch. Ten minutes later the guard led Isaac in. He slithered into the chair across from John.

"I'm Detective John Stark. My daughter, Kira, was at your farm."

"Nice piece," Isaac grinned. "You do good work."

John's hands clenched on the table.

"I like to test out my merchandise before making a sale. I think that's only fair, don't you?"

Griff reached over and took my hand, holding it tight between both of his.

"I don't give a rat's ass about how you do business," John said. "I want my daughter back and you're gonna tell me how to find her."

"If only it were that easy. Once my girls leave my home I don't know where they go."

"Who's Lucas?"

"Never heard of him."

"Bullshit. We have eyewitness information regarding everyone and everything that went on at *Oracles of the Kingdom.*"

Isaac laughed. "Now it's my turn. Bullshit."

I pulled my hand out of Griff's. "I'm going in there."

"John's doing fine."

"But Isaac doesn't believe him. If he sees me, he'll know he's screwed. He might talk."

"You're not going in there. It's too soon for you to confront him."

I moved past him and opened the door.

"You're making a mistake," Griff said.

In the hallway I put my hand on the knob of the interrogation room door and took a breath. Isaac was as low as they come. He'd gotten the better of me once, but it wouldn't happen again. He looked up when I opened the door. The surprise on his face was worth the risk of confronting him and gave me an immediate upper hand. My heart slowed.

"No, not bullshit," I said. "He does know everything about the farm."

Isaac's recovery was seamless. "Yeah? Does he know what a good lay his informant is?"

I thought of Griff listening from the other side of the glass. My stomach knotted.

"Does he know you like it doggie style? Oh, Mama, that soft, white ass."

Tears stung my eyes.

"Enough." John stood, his chair flipped backward and clanged onto the cement floor. He grabbed Isaac by the hair and pressed his face into the table.

The cop in the corner cleared his throat and shuffled foot to foot.

"You open your mouth again and I'll drive your face through the metal. You got it?" Isaac nodded as best he could under John's hold. John looked at me. "Out," he said.

I turned without a word and left the room. Griff was waiting in the hallway. He didn't say anything just guided me back into the observation room so we could listen to the rest of John's interview.

"Griff…" I said once he'd closed the door.

He held his hand up and shook his head. "I told you not to do it."

"I thought I could help."

"You can. Just not like that."

"You don't have to get pissed. I was trying to…" My voice cracked and I stopped. "I'm sorry that you had to hear that."

He turned and his face softened when he looked at me. "I'm not pissed, but we have to treat this like any other case. We can't get tangled up in emotions right now. How we feel about what you went through has to wait if we're going to be of any help to John."

I leaned against the wall beside the door and closed my eyes. I wasn't very good at compartmentalizing. If something was making me crazy I couldn't set it aside until the moment was right. "If this relationship is too much...I mean If you can't be with me because...because of..."

"Britt." His voice was stern. "I'm not saying we won't talk about what happened or that I don't think about it all the time, but right now our heads have to be in the game. We have a lifetime to work through it, but we have to find Kira now." He turned back to watch John and Isaac.

"So maybe that bitch told you a few things," Isaac said.

"She can positively ID every person that attended your little party. We've arrested everyone from the Chief of Police to town officials and your doctor friend. The party's over Bennett, best thing you can do for yourself is talk. I want Lucas. I don't give a shit about you. You're small beans. Give me Lucas and I'll recommend a deal."

"What kind of deal?"

"That's not up to me."

"I have to think about it."

John stood. "Don't think too long. If someone talks before you do, the offer's gone."

John left Isaac sitting at the table and met us in the hallway. "What the hell were you thinking coming in there?"

"I wanted him to know you weren't lying, that you did have all the information on him."

"At your own expense?"

"Status quo."

"I'm sorry," John said.

"Don't be. I'm beyond it. He can't hurt me anymore." I thought about my little melt down with Griff. Okay, so maybe I wasn't beyond it. Chances were good that I never would be, but something positive had to come out of this mess. If it wouldn't be my self-worth, then it would be John's daughter. Who knew, maybe we still had a shot at both.

"Well you sure as hell got his attention," John said. "That much was obvious. He knows we have him. Let him chew on that for a while."

"You want Stebbins?" Merridan offered.

"I'll give it a try if it's okay with you."

"He hasn't talked to us. Maybe you'll have better luck."

Griff and I made a food run while John talked with Stebbins and we met back at the car for the rest of the trip.

"Get anywhere with Stebbins?" Griff asked handing John a brown bag, dark with grease.

"Only thing that came out of his mouth was the name of his lawyer."

"His lawyer is probably one of Isaac's clients too."

"That's my bet," John said. He reached into his lunch bag, drew out a handful of fries then pulled back onto the highway toward Edmundston.

Grand Falls was forty miles from the border crossing at Edmundston. We pulled into the precinct's parking lot and I rubbed my sweaty palms against my jeans for the hundredth time. On the sidewalk in front of the police department John stopped. "A number of small towns fall under Grand Falls PD's jurisdiction, including Saint-Leonard," he said looking at me.

I nodded. "You mean these cops oversee Rusty's."

"Oversee or partake. Some of these guys will be more than happy when this is over and the bar's back in business. Keep that in mind. Any information they give us we take with a grain of salt until we know who's who."

Inside, the station was the picture of work ethic. No feet up on desks, uniforms pressed and clean, everyone focused and not a doughnut in sight. Un-American. The staff sergeant at the desk directed us down a hallway to Chief LeBlanc's office. On our left, doors led into conference rooms and offices. On our right, was an open view of the bullpen. Cops of various levels working on assignment. I adjusted my baseball hat a little further down over my face. It was unlikely that I'd run into the cop who'd known Julia at Rusty's and even if I did I didn't think he'd recognize me out of context. It would be one of those, *"Don't I know you from somewhere?"* I hoped he wouldn't connect the dots.

Chief of Police LeBlanc rose to meet us as we came through his office door. He extended a hand to John. "Nice to see you again, Detective Stark." He nodded to Griff and then looked at me. "And you must be the brave young woman I've been hearing about." He took my hand in both of his. "It's my pleasure to meet the heroine," he said.

"That's a little pre-mature."

"You're right, Mademoiselle Callahan there's more to do, but you've accomplished much in the past few weeks."

I decided to ignore John's grain of salt idea when it came to Chief LeBlanc.

"Have a seat," he said.

I glanced around the room at the buttery, leather furniture. The Canadian government knew how to take care of their men in blue.

"I'm sorry to have to tell you that Monsieur Tuton has refused to speak."

"Monsieur Tuton?" I asked.

"I believe you know him as Clive."

"What about Myles?"

"A few of the paying customers, the bar owner and Monsieur Tuton were the only arrests made. Who is Myles?"

"Clive's partner."

"It seems he has escaped us, for now."

"Did you offer Tuton a deal?' John asked.

LeBlanc turned to John. "Not yet. This case changed hands at the border and is now under my jurisdiction, but I know you have a lot at stake, Detective. I hope we can work on this together in ways that will satisfy us both."

I glanced at Griff and smiled, impressed. Etiquette like this was a lost art in the U.S. Maybe this guy could teach us a thing or two.

"I appreciate that," John said. "I assume any deal in exchange for information has to be approved by your DA. Sorry, what's the correct title in Canada?"

"Chief Crown Prosecutor. That would be, Madame Renault. I have already arranged a meeting for later today."

"Would you object to my speaking with Clive Touton?"

"That can be arranged. I will have one of my investigators accompany you."

"First I'd like to go to his house and then take a look at the bar. See what I come up with."

"Those locations are still considered crime scenes. I'm sure you're aware of the necessary precautions."

John held up his hands. "Won't touch a thing."

LeBlanc nodded. "I have units stationed at both places. I'll radio them that you're coming. They can escort you."

"Appreciate it," John said.

"Our IT department is going through the laptop we recovered from the house. They will contact me the moment they have something."

"Good. We'll do some sightseeing and reconvene this afternoon."

"Very good, Detective. I'll be here."

We left Chief LeBlanc and took our places back in John's Suburban. I dreaded like hell going back to Clive's house and facing that basement again. But what had LeBlanc called me, a heroine? Who was I to ruin his fantasy? I made a fist, digging my nails into the palm of my hand. I could do it. I would do it.

"Why's LeBlanc so agreeable?" I asked.

"He's just as aware as we are that some of his men frequent Rusty's. Hell, he may even be a regular himself. He'll happily help us as long as we don't dig too deep into the clientele."

"And will we?"

"His men are his problem. I just want my daughter back."

Following the directions LeBlanc gave us we took a right out of the parking lot, followed Main Street five miles out of town heading back the way we'd come. At a flashing yellow light we took a left. At the next intersection my stomach landed in my throat. A blue lettered sign hung out over the sidewalk, *Campbell's Bakery*.

"That's..." I pointed to the sign.

Griff nodded. "I see it."

John took another left. Three story row houses on either side of the street blended one into the next, nondescript. Halfway down on the right, yellow police tape set one off from the rest. John eased the car to a stop in front and my heart started beating a hole through my chest.

Griff turned toward me from the passenger seat in front. "You don't have to come in."

"Yes I do," I said and stepped out of the vehicle on shaky legs.

Five metal steps led to the front door. The door that Clive had led me through the night I'd arrived. Beside them, six cement steps descended to the basement. John pulled the keys that LeBlanc had given him from his pocket and tore back the yellow tape from across the stairs and chose the basement.

"There're no windows in here," I said as he pushed open the door.

Griff tried the light switch to his left and the naked overhead bulb gave us 20-watt voltage. John switched on his flashlight. I sucked in a breath as the room lit up. Filthy mattresses lined the floor. A few scrunched up bags from Campbell's lay scattered on top. There was a pair of jeans and one lone sock to my right. The room still held the odor of women, unwashed women. I felt Griff's eyes on me and turned my head not wanting to see the look on his face.

"Jesus," John said more to himself than to us. "I'm sorry, Callahan."

I nodded, not trusting my voice.

"She was here?"

"Yeah, she was here."

"How long?"

"Ruth said Lucas took her from the farm roughly a month before I got there. So, she arrived here three or four weeks before I did. She was upstairs with Myles when I first arrived then he…he…" I stopped, remembering the way he'd thrown her from the top step when he'd finished with her. "Then she came down here with the rest of us," I said.

I could see the pain in John's eyes at my words. It was my turn to be sorry.

"There's nothing here for us," he said. "Let's take a look upstairs. He led us up the wooden steps.

I stopped for a moment at the bottom remembering lying there and believing in that moment that I'd never see Griff again then I'd put my hand on the Campbell's bag and life took a turn. Out of the depths, I thought, and joined them in the kitchen.

John was opening and closing drawers. Griff had ventured into the living room. I stepped onto the Oriental carpet and an image flashed in my head of Clive beating the crap out of me. I pushed it away fast. I was working hard to block any memory of this place. Adopting Griff's tactic of temporary denial, but he must have seen something on my face because when I looked up he was staring at me.

"You okay?" he asked.

"Yeah, I'm good."

John rustled through a few more drawers and Griff and I headed for the stairs. I followed him up to the third floor. He stepped into the bathroom where Julia and Kira and I had showered. Where I'd told Kira that we'd get out, together.

"We showered in here," I said looking inside the stall. Mildew crept up the walls growing out of soap scum thick as cream. I'd never noticed it before, never looked this closely, but now standing here with Griff I felt ashamed. As if I were somehow responsible for the vile appearance of the house.

Griff looked at me but didn't speak.

"I told Kira she'd be okay. I told her we'd stick together...."

"Don't go there, Britt."

"LeBlanc thinks I'm a hero. I'm nowhere close. I'm a liar and a traitor. And now Kira's lost to us because I fucked up."

"Britt, stop." Griff took my elbow and turned me toward him. "You did everything you could. John's closer than he's ever been because of you. And we're not leaving until we find her."

"You okay, Callahan?" John was standing outside the door.

I pulled my arm away from Griff. "I'm fine."

"You don't look like it. You want to go to the motel? I can drop you there before we go to the bar."

"Good idea," Griff said.

"No. I'm going with you." I brushed past them both and walked down the stairs. In the kitchen I hesitated in front of the basement steps then I descended, moving over the mattresses with my eyes straight ahead and my mind blank. Reaching John's car, I felt like I'd just run the gauntlet. I leaned against it and breathed in cool air while John locked up the house.

"We're heading to Rusty's," John said and glanced at me through the rear view mirror as though giving me one more chance to opt out. I nodded and he pulled away from the curb.

Like the house, the bar's front door was blocked by yellow police tape. And like the house, John tore it away, inserted a key and we stepped inside. The smell of stale bear and cigarettes was enough to gag us. Griff wandered down the hall to the bathrooms while John went behind the bar. Again I followed Griff. We stepped inside the ladies room. The window was still broken. I could see bits of dried blood where I'd scraped my stomach sliding out. I pointed to it. "Kira's and my attempt," I said. "That's what did us in. Myles was waiting outside with a rifle." I touched the side of my head.

"There's nothing in here," Griff said and ushered me out.

We stepped back into the main room. "John?" Griff called.

"In here."

We followed his voice to the room behind the bar. Rusty's room. The room where I'd...

"What a dump," John said. "With all the goddamn money these guys are making off the backs of young girls...these conditions...they're...I wouldn't put a fucking animal through what we've seen today." He picked up a chair and slammed it against the wall.

Back at the station, we met LeBlanc in his office.

"How did your tour go?" he asked.

John shrugged. "Depressing, to put it mildly."

LeBlanc nodded. "I was left with the same impression when I made the rounds myself. Do you wish to speak with Clive?"

"Might as well," John said.

"And you won't tear his head from his body," Griff asked. "If you're alone with him?"

"I'm not making any promises," John said as we left LeBlanc's office to go to the holding area.

Griff and I stepped into the observation room and watched John on the other side of the glass. Clive was already seated, his hands cuffed behind his back. His hair hung in greasy strands around his face. His right knee bounced beneath the table. John took the chair across from him.

Griff reached over and took my hand. "You're a tough cookie, Callahan."

For the first time that day, I smiled.

"So you're Daddy?" Clive laughed.

I flinched at the sound of his voice.

"Where is she?"

Clive sneered. "Sold to the highest bidder by now."

"You give me Lucas, I'll see to it that you get a deal."

"Lucas who?" Clive sneered.

"Don't be an ass. I've talked with Bennett. I know Lucas is the middleman. He's the one I want. You and Bennett don't mean shit to me. You're sweat on a slug's testicles and I don't stoop that low."

I laughed. It felt good. "Do slugs even have testicles?"

Griff shook his head. "Damned if I know. First time I've heard that one."

"I ain't givin' you shit, Pop. You're wasting your time."

John stood and pushed his chair in then leaned across the table into Clive's face. "You and Bennett are too stupid to know when your ass is fried and when it's time to save yourselves. But you know what? I'm glad you're that dumb because when I get Lucas without you, you're both gonna fry for what you've done."

"No death penalty in Canada," Clive said.

"Who said anything about the death penalty? Guys who will take you out in exchange for reduced time are a dime a dozen. Hell, I'll cite them for good behavior."

Clive didn't say anything, but the muscles in his jaw were working overtime.

We met John in the hallway. "Slug testicles?" I asked.

"You liked that one, Callahan?" He looked pleased. "I kind of liked it myself. Came out of nowhere."

"Creative," Griff said.

We made plans to meet LeBlanc in the morning and retreated to the motel. After a shower, I wrapped myself in a towel and joined Griff for some mindless television.

"Did you think it was a waste of time to go through the house and the bar today?" I asked him. "I mean the Grand Falls police already did it. The only thing they found was the computer. That's probably our only hope of finding anything."

"I think John needed to see where Kira had been. It gave him a sense of being close to her. It's the first time he's felt that in a long time."

"But I think it made him crazy to see the conditions she was living in."

"It couldn't have been easy for you either."

"It sucked."

He stroked my hair back from my face and kissed my cheek. "What can I do?"

"Nothing. Just be here."

Griff turned off the T.V. and the light and I rolled into his arms. I lay tight against him, chest to chest, my face buried in his neck.

WEDNESDAY

Business was well under way at the police department when we arrived the next morning.

"Help yourself," the desk sergeant said, motioning us toward a table in the corner with a Keurig coffee maker and a box of croissants.

I was starving and didn't hesitate. With a hazelnut K-cup brewing, I bit into a chocolate filled croissant and put another one on a paper plate.

"Hungry?" Griff asked coming up beside me and helping himself.

John made a cup of coffee and we followed him to LeBlanc's office. He was hunched over his desk with a uniform from the IT department. He glanced up and nodded as we came into the room.

"Officer DeBolt has been working all night and it's paid off," he said.

"What have you got?" John asked stepping up behind them both.

"It's the emails," DeBolt said. "There are a number of them to someone named Lucas. Most of the conversations are in code, like this one says, "Tonight I will deliver 3 ducks to "Bon Sejour". Bon Sejour is the repeating phrase in most of the emails and the rest of the message applies to food orders, pick-ups or deliveries."

"The girls?" John asked.

"That's what I'm thinking," LeBlanc said.

"What the hell is Bon Sejour?" John asked.

"It's a restaurant in Edmundston. The name means pleasant journey. It's the kind of place you go for a special night out like an anniversary or birthday. Not your everyday lunch spot."

"Well, it's our lunch spot today." John looked at Griff and me.

"Good," I said biting into my second croissant. "I'm starving."

At 11:30 the maître d' at Bon Sejour seated us at a corner table in the elegant dining room. The lighting was dim despite elaborate chandeliers overhead. He lit the candle at the center of our table after handing us black leather menus.

"Something to drink?"

"Ice tea all the way around," John said without giving us the opportunity to get something stronger, which I'd definitely planned on. I was worried that Bon Sejour was a side job for Lucas or even Myles, and the thought of running into one of them had me salivating for a shot of Oban.

I ordered Escargot. Griff and John went for steaks and since I'm not much for red meat, I refused to exchange a snail for beef, not even one. Too many bagels had made me as food aggressive as a stray dog.

There was a minimal crew on in the middle of the day and the restaurant was less than half full. A three-martini lunch crowd in business suites and a few well-to-do, seventyish women dined alongside us. The cronies' perfume defeated any hope of enjoying the savory aromas floating from the kitchen. Griff and John surveyed the room. "I'm not getting much of a vibe about this place," Griff said. "You think this was also code for somewhere else? I can't see Clive spending time here."

"No, but maybe Lucas," John said. He looked at me. "Would Lucas fit in here?"

I thought of him standing in Isaac's front hall in his black leather jacket. He had European good looks and a Frenchman's charm. I nodded. "Definitely."

"But the patrons don't look like they'd do business with Clive or Isaac.

"I think Lucas is a few rungs up the ladder," John said. "And his clients are above that."

"That's why Clive needs a deal he can't say no to," John said. "We have to get to Lucas. Hopefully Madame Renault will see it that way too."

Madame Renault's office was as productive as the Grand Falls PD. "These Canadians like to work," I said to John as we followed her secretary into a high ceilinged, oak trimmed office.

Madame Renault looked up from her desk where she was dwarfed by stacks of vanilla colored files. Chief LeBlanc crossed the room first, his hand extended.

"Chief, nice to see you." Madame Renault came around her desk and shook the Chief's hand.

"This is Detective John Stark," he said turning her attention to us. "And this is Griff Cole and Britt Callahan, PIs helping with the case."

"A sex trafficking case, correct?"

"Seems to be turning into that," John said. "I was looking for my daughter in Maine. She's been missing for some time. That led us here, to Clive Tuton. From what we have so far, he's buying and selling young girls."

"And he's not talking." Madame Renault said.

"That's why we're here." Chief LeBlanc folded his arms over his chest. "My IT specialist has come up with some information that could be valuable, but we need Clive to decipher it. We'd like to offer him a deal if he'll name his middleman. If we can find him, he'll take us to the top."

"I don't want to give this guy anything less than he has coming, believe me," John interrupted. "But at this point, I think it's our only shot at making headway."

"What do you have in mind?"

"I don't know much about Canadian law. I'll defer to you," John said. "Trafficking in Canada is huge. Unfortunately, we have not scored well according to The Future Group's report in our attempts to confront the problem, but we are addressing it. The minimum sentence for trafficking is five years. The maximum can go up to twenty. It has a lot to do with the ages of the victims. Prostitution by willing adults is a different matter. How old are the women in question?"

Griff and John looked at me."

"I was sold to Clive Tuton," I said stepping forward. "I'm thirty-three, but he thought I was ten years younger. Most of the girls I saw were over eighteen, but not all. John's daughter, is eighteen now, but was fifteen when she went missing."

Madame Renault nodded. "I can offer him seven years if he gives you what you want. Otherwise, tell Tuton that I'll recommend the longest the judge will allow."

As we turned to leave, the Crown Prosecutor touched my arm. "I'm sorry for what you've been through. Chief LeBlanc filled me in on the work you've done. You're a brave woman."

There it was again, someone mistaking me for a person with guts. I wanted to point out that I was here and Kira was still there. So what did that say?

Back at the station Detective Carver accompanied John into the interrogation room. John took a seat across from Clive while Carver hung back, leaning against the wall. Griff and I watched from the other side of the glass.

"I'm not doing seven years," Clive said. "Are you crazy?"

"We have you. We have the girls that you had at your house. We have your computer. And as promised by the Chief Crown Prosecutor you'll do a lot more than seven years if you keep your mouth shut."

"The girls will not speak against me. They liked their work. I did nothing to them. They were legal age."

"Not all of them."

Clive shrugged. "You don't know that."

"I'm going in," I said to Griff.

"No you're not. It didn't work the last time. It won't work this time."

"I can do it this time. I'm practicing temporary denial," I said quoting him.

"Britt, don't do it to yourself. John can handle it."

"If I tell him who I am, he'll know John has him."

I stepped into the hallway drawing in and releasing a breath as deeply as I could, the way a meditation instructor once showed me. 'It introduces calm into the body,' she'd said. Calm was a new concept for my body. I tried it again. Elusive. I gave up, opened the door to the interrogation room and stepped inside.

Carver wrapped his hand around my elbow, holding me back.

John looked at me, grimaced and then nodded to Carver.

Willing my voice not to shake, I approached the table. "Hello Clive, my name is Britt Callahan. I'm a PI working with the Portland, Maine Criminal Investigation Unit.".

A compilation of shock, surprise and fear overtook his smug grin. The adrenalin started in my chest and made its way to my head, flushing my cheeks and making my neck tingle. I had the upper hand. He was the loser here, not me.

"I understand you've been offered a deal. I think it would be wise of you to take it," I said. "If you don't," I put my palms on the table and leaned toward him. "If you don't, I will bring to light every tiny detail, every word spoken, every minute of the time I spent in your basement and with my testimony, I will bury you as far into the prison system as is humanly possible." I turned and walked back to the door, opened it and stepped into the hallway.

"Nicely done, partner," Griff said coming up to me with a grin.

I held out my hand. "Not even a tremor." For the first time in weeks I almost felt like myself.

The door behind us opened and we both turned to John and Carver coming out of the interrogation room. John looked at me and smiled. "We got it. Well, you did. He knew we had him. Seven years suddenly sounded good."

"So what'd he say?" Griff asked.

"It's the restaurant. It's a front. Well, let's put it this way. Food is sold in front. Girls are sold out back. It's where we hook up with Lucas. "

"How do we do that?" Griff asked.

"There should be a white card in with Clive's stuff. Cops must have whatever was in his wallet when they brought him in."

"I'll bring it to LeBlanc's office," Detective Carver said taking off down the hallway.

"The white card is the ticket in," John said. "When it's presented at the restaurant, it gets you in as a bidder on the girls."

"The girls are at the restaurant?"

"Not there, but not far. The card gets you out back where you bid on girls via computer image. If you're the high bidder then you make arrangements to pick the girl up at a location they arrange."

"Does he know if Kira's one of these girls?" Griff asked.

John nodded. "It's where Lucas said he was taking her. He gets a cut of what the girls make. It's big money according to dipshit in there." John nodded to the interrogation room where Clive was waiting to be taken back to his cell.

"So now what?" Griff asked.

"I'll go talk with LeBlanc," John said. "It's his party. Let's hope we're on the guest list,"

"I'm making the bid?" Griff asked as we walked into LeBlanc's office.

"When Kira sees you, she'll know she's safe," LeBlanc said and my men are better used at Bon Sejour. That's where the action will be. I'll have Detective Carver and a detail follow you to the pick-up location. As soon as you have her we'll take down the restaurant."

"Go get some clothes." John handed Griff a credit card. "It's the department's so don't have too much fun, but you need to look like the sky's the limit, 'cause it will be. I'm this close. I'm not losing her again. Do your shopping and meet me back here. I'm going to hammer out the details with LeBlanc. His guys will run the show when it comes to breaking open the restaurant and making arrests, the three of us will focus on Kira."

Edmundston was the closest place to find a men's clothing store that didn't advertise Carhart as their primary line. The tri-fold directory just inside the mall's entrance told us that Brooks Brothers was located right beside Sam's Smoke Shop.

"Now that's fate. I haven't had a Honey Berry in weeks."

"So what's a few more?" Griff asked.

"Oh no, this is an omen. You go to Brooks Brothers to change your persona while I go to Sam's and indulge mine."

We located the stores and I slipped into the smoke shop with the promise of meeting Griff, ASAP. He rolled his eyes and left me at the door. There was no smoking in the mall so I pocketed my purchase, smiling with the anticipation of a kid on Christmas Eve.

Griff was standing in front of a mannequin in the suit department. I came up beside him and checked out the ensemble in front of us. Charcoal gray suit, pale pink shirt, the tie held various shades of gray with a pink splash, a matching ascot in the pocket.

"What do you think?" He asked.

"Nice. Says money, but quietly."

"Can I help you?" A salesman asked slipping up beside us.

"I'll take that," Griff said to him.

With some tape measuring magic the sales clerk had everything wrapped and ready to go within fifteen minutes.

"Men are so easy," I said lingering next to John's Suburban, savoring the Honey Berry I'd lit the moment we stepped outside. "It would have taken me at least two hours to figure out the look I'd need if I was going in there tonight."

"That's why you're not," Griff said. "Put that thing out. We've got to go."

I ignored his request and took another drag, filling my mouth with the sweet taste of blackberries. "That's not the reason I'm not going in."

"I know," he said. Then recognizing my insecurity, added. "It's got nothing to do with competence. If Myles or Lucas saw you it would blow the whole thing."

"So you know it's not 'cause I couldn't do it."

He cocked his head. "Callahan, after what you've done I'd put my money on you every time." He put his finger under my chin, tipped my face to his and kissed me. "Jesus, throw that thing out, will you?"

Satisfied, I ground the cigar underfoot and opened the car door.

It was seven o'clock when we walked into the Chief's office. He and John were bent over the desk.

"Get everything you needed?" John asked glancing up.

"I'll be King of the Prom," Griff said raising the suit bag he held in his hand.

"Go get dressed. We'll have you wired and there by nine."

"You driving?"

"Got you a rental, Mercedes Sport."

Griff let out a whistle, "Like your style."

"You gotta look the part. According to Clive these are the big spenders."

Griff left the room to change and I stepped up beside John to see what the two men were studying. A blueprint for Bon Sejour lay across the desk. The main dining area was easy to see as was the bar, but extending from the back of the kitchen was a long hallway with a number of small rooms off each side.

"Looks like this is where the deals are made." LeBlanc tapped his index finger on the map. "There's a back door at the end of this hall leading outside so nobody retraces their steps. You make your bid and leave out the back. Happily if you're the high bidder."

"He's gonna have to be tonight," John added.

The door opened and Griff stepped in.

"Good choice," John said eyeing him up and down. "You'll have their attention."

"Are you implying that I look hot?"

John gave him a half smile. "Closest you'll ever get. Now take your shirt off."

"No dinner first?" Griff asked.

LeBlanc picked up his desk phone. "We're ready," he said.

Not a minute later a man came into the office holding the gear that would connect Griff to John and me waiting in a car outside. If all went well, Griff would be the high bidder on Kira and John and I would follow him along with Detective Carver and a couple of uniforms to the designated pick up spot. Once Griff had Kira safely in hand, it would be a shit show at Bon Sejour as cops descended on the restaurant and a horror for Lucas or whoever the middleman was that brought Kira. If things didn't go as hoped, at least they could bust the restaurant and hopefully we'd get a lead on Kira's whereabouts. The wire ran through the seam of Griff's shirt and ended in a tiny microphone clipped inside the ascot. That way, Griff could still open his shirt on the off chance that someone checked and he'd be clean.

"Put this in your wallet," LeBlanc said handing him an all white piece of plastic, the size of a driver's license.

"What the hell's this?" Griff asked turning the card over in his hand.

"Your ticket in."

"There's nothing on it."

"Encrypted, I assume. Tuton said to hand it to the maître d' as soon as you go in the door. He'll seat you at the bar. They'll come for you when the bidding starts. My guess is that you'll go into one of those small rooms. There're six of them. Six men bidding at the same time, but you won't see each other."

"We'll be listening outside," John said. "You need to tell us what's happening, but there may be someone in the room with you. If you don't see Kira, tell them you don't see anything interesting. That's our queue. We'll bring the house down. If you do see her, say you like the blonde. No one else will do. Callahan and I will be waiting outside to escort you to the pick-up. It's off-sight. We'll have plenty of back up. As soon as Lucas brings Kira out, the Canadian force will be on him like flies on shit."

"Appropriate description," I said.

John tossed Griff the keys to the rented Mercedes.

Griff fisted the keys in one hand and laid the other on John's shoulder. "We're gonna get her," he said.

We watched Griff enter the restaurant from a darkened alleyway across the street. Bon Sejour was surrounded on four sides by unmarked police cruisers. Whether or not we got Kira, this was going to be a huge bust. The door closed behind Griff and my stomach dropped.

I was starting to wonder if the wire was working when I heard a voice. "This way Monsieur."

Scuffling, then, "Something to drink?"

"Glenlivet rocks," Griff said.

We sat in silence listening to the tinkling of ice cubes and glasses. Some pleasantries were exchanged as someone took a seat beside Griff. I was getting antsy waiting. My palms were sweaty and I rubbed them down my thighs drying them against my jeans.

"Anxious?" John asked.

I nodded.

"Last time I saw Kira, she was fifteen." He looked down at the steering wheel and ran his palm around it. "Alexis had been dead two weeks. Kira screamed at me that it was my fault her mother died. Said she hated me. Said I hadn't taken good enough care of her mom. Kira thought she should have had a nurse or been in a hospital somewhere, but Alexis and I had talked about it. She wanted to die with me, in her own house, in her own bed. But it cost me my daughter. Neither one of us saw that coming. But you know?" He turned to look at me. "I don't think we would have changed a thing. Just maybe tried to explain it to Kira better than we did so she would have understood. We thought we were protecting her."

I laid my hand on John's arm. "She doesn't feel that way anymore. She wants to get home to you as much as you want her back."

A voice cut into our conversation. "This way, sir."

My adrenalin spiked and I leaned forward straining to hear every detail. It sucked not seeing what was happening. A door opened, scuffling, then closed.

"Have a seat." It was the same voice.

"He must be in one of the rooms," John said his strained posture matching my own.

"No, not that one," Griff said.

John and I looked at each other. Griff was viewing the girls.

"No," Griff said again.

"A man who knows what he wants," the voice said and gave a soft laugh. "That can make things easier, but more often harder. Sometimes you should just take whatever's offered."

"I didn't come here for conversation," Griff said. "Show me another."

John nodded. "Good," he said more to himself than to me.

"Yes," Griff said. "That one. I like the blonde."

My heart somersaulted. I looked at John, but he was staring out the windshield nodding his head.

"She's been bid on already," the voice said.

"Then go higher," Griff answered.

"How much?"

"Another thousand."

"As you wish," the voice said and then, "The other bidder has upped you by five hundred dollars."

"Another thousand," Griff said. "No one else will do."

John drew a deep breath. "C'mon, man."

We sat in silence, waiting.

"She's yours, sir," the voice said.

John smacked the steering wheel with his hand and started the car. "We're almost there, Callahan."

"These are your directions to the pick-up location," the man said. "There will be someone there to meet you. I'll escort you outside, sir."

A minute later Griff appeared from the side of the building and walked to the white Mercedes Sport parked at the curb. As soon as the car door closed his voice came over the wire. "The directions are to a place called "Lands End".

John called LeBlanc and told him the meet was at a place called Lands End.

"It's a motel just this side of Edmundston, ten miles, give or take," LeBlanc said. "Detective Carver will lead you there. I'll wait here for your go on the restaurant. Good luck."

A nondescript sedan pulled out of the street beside us. Griff fell in behind it and John and I behind him. Two cruisers followed. LeBlanc wanted this as much as we did so there was no shortage of backup. He and the rest of the task force would seize the restaurant the moment we had Kira in hand. If they went in too soon whoever was with Kira could be tipped off and abort the meeting. The restaurant had to be secondary to getting Kira. I gave LeBlanc credit for agreeing to let it go down that way. He must have kids.

We left the lights of Main Street behind us and drove through a small suburban outlay, from there we moved steadily into nothing. Not a house or a streetlight, not even another car. We'd been driving about twenty minutes when the lead car dropped back and waved Griff past. Another mile and Griff put on his right blinker. I couldn't see anything at first and then a solitary light appeared through the overhanging branches along the side of the road. Detective Carver in the unmarked cruiser ahead of us pulled over and doused his lights. We pulled in behind him. Up ahead, I watched Griff make a right turn into the parking lot.

John put down his window and Carver approached.

"Who the hell puts a motel out here in the middle of nowhere?" John asked.

"Used to draw tourists from the border crossing, but most folks head on toward Quebec now. I wondered how this place stayed afloat. Guess I have my answer." Carver raised the zipper on his jacket and removed a pair of leather gloves from one pocket. We go on foot from here," he said.

One of the cruisers was idling behind us. The other had stopped just beyond the motel's entrance. We left the car and started through the trees coming up on the side of the building. It was a two-story structure with six windows on each floor. Two of the rooms were lit on the upper level, one on the first floor. The Mercedes Griff had been driving was parked in front of number 5. A lamp inside lit a gold semi-circle on the asphalt beside the car. Overhead, the moon drifted in and out from behind thick gray rain clouds, alternately showing us our surroundings and then casting us into darkness. I reached my hand around to the back of my jeans and felt my Pink Lady tucked in tight. Griff hadn't asked and I hadn't volunteered that I was carrying. Like he'd said, better safe than sorry.

Carver stuck out his hand slowing us down. Then motioned for me to come up beside him. We stoop walked across the parking lot and hugged the side of the building inching our way toward number 5. When we were outside the window Carver leaned his head to view the room then nodded for me to do the same. I could hear their voices and knew without looking who it was.

"You have my goods?" Griff asked.

Lucas laughed. "So that's what Americans call this. Exchanging goods? I like it." He held up a cell phone. "She's all yours. Everything's in order I've been told." He smacked the back of his hand against the bathroom door. "Hurry up. I'm a busy man. You're not the only delivery I have tonight."

Kira stepped into the room.

I turned to LeBlanc. "Lucas," I whispered.

"You're sure?"

I nodded.

We ran silently back to the trees where John and the uniformed cops waited. Carver motioned for two of the cops to go with him back across the parking lot to the door. Two more went to the front of the building. It was hard to say if this place had interior doors or a lobby, but if it did we'd be covered. Stark and I broke to the right moving silently through the darkness under an umbrella of trees. Fire regulations would mean a back entrance. Whether or not the motel was up to code was another question.

Before we'd all reached our designated positions the door opened and Lucas stepped out. Griff and Kira were behind him. Lucas saw Carver coming halfway across the parking lot and broke to his left. Consumed by the shadows of the upper level walkway, he ran the length of the building. Griff pushed Kira back inside the room and took off after him, but he didn't make it far. At the end of the building, before disappearing into the woods Lucas turned and got off one shot. Griff went down hard on the cement.

I ran for Griff. John was on my heels but diverted into room number 5. I hit the asphalt beside Griff as Carver and the rest disappeared into the trees after Lucas. I knelt beside Griff and lifted his head onto my lap, repeating his name over and over. His eyes were barely open, but they found my voice. He looked up and tried to speak. I covered the hole in the center of his chest with my hand. His blood was warm as it seeped through my fingers.

"Shhh," I told him, kissing his face, my tears on his cheeks. "Don't say anything."

"Daddy, Daddy." I could hear Kira crying and then John was beside me holding her against him. "Is he...?"

"He's breathing," I told him.

"Stay here with Britt," John said to Kira and took off, following Carver into the darkness.

I could see waves of light splashing over the trees as the cops searched the surrounding woods for Lucas. Four shots rang out.

"Britt?" Kira knelt beside me. "How did you...how..."

I handed her my cell phone. "Call for an ambulance, hurry." I gave her the address Griff had given us and listened as she relayed the information into the phone. Griff was motionless in my arms, but blood pulsed through my fingers so his heart was still beating.

Leaves rustled and twigs snapped to my left. I looked up expecting John or Carver as a figure broke from the trees and ran toward us. As it neared, I recognized the build and then the face as it came into view. It was Lucas.

"You fucking bitch," he said, when he got closer. "I should have killed you a long time ago." He pulled his car keys from his pants' pocket.

"You're surrounded by cops," I said.

"Your cops are off chasing their shadows," he laughed, coming closer. "Is he dead?" He was no more than three feet away.

"No."

"Not yet." He turned and started walking toward his car.

I watched him moving away from me and remembered how he'd called me trash the night we crossed the border and punched me in the face. I remembered Isaac raping me as he held me over the washing machine in the basement. I thought of Julia, Ruth, Elizabeth, Kira and the thousands of girls whose lives had been destroyed by men like him. I let Griff slip from my lap and rose to my knees. Reaching back, I drew out my Pink Lady and repeated Griff's words. *"It's not so hard, just aim and shoot."*

He was almost to his car.

"Hey, Lucas," I said.

He turned, looked surprised when he saw the gun and then laughed. "You? You're just a whore."

I stared into is eyes, hoped my aim was true and pulled the trigger.

At first he didn't move, just stared back at me like he couldn't believe I'd done it. A thin line of blood ran from the hole in his forehead down his nose and chin. It splashed onto the front of his shirt. In slow motion with his eyes still on me, he dropped to his knees and then, after a second or two fell forward. His face bounced off the pavement once and then he was still.

Beneath me, Griff stirred. John and Carver burst out of the trees. They stopped about six feet away and took in the scene.

Before anyone spoke, Kira was on her feet running to John.

John looked from Lucas to me and nodded.

An ambulance screeched into the parking lot. It's lights flashing. Two EMTs jumped from the truck.

"This one first." John pointed to Griff and lifted me from the ground. He pried open my fingers and took the .38 out of my hand. "Jesus Christ, Callahan," he said shaking his head and looking at the piece. "Pink?"

I was watching them load Griff into the ambulance and wanted to laugh at the absurdity of a pink gun, but couldn't.

"That was one hell of a shot," John said. "Now go." He pushed me toward the ambulance.

I glanced at Lucas face down on the parking lot and felt nothing but satisfaction. Carver was talking fast into his cell phone to Chief LeBlanc at Bon Sejour. "It's a go," he said. "Now. Now."

An EMT helped me inside the ambulance. I sat on a low bench beside Griff. The door slammed shut. "Gunshot wound to the chest," the driver said into his radio. "Stable. We're on our way."

The siren came to life and we started to move. Out the back window I saw Kira rest her head on John's shoulder. Their arms were securely around each other, neither one in any hurry to let go.

THREE WEEKS LATER

It was mid-February, but the temperature read forty-eight degrees. In Maine, a day like this is both a tease and a gift. And we were taking advantage of it. The window was open a crack, but it was enough for the breeze to cause Griff's shirt to flutter. The skin on his chest was still tinted light purple. It had faded significantly from the deep plum it had been except at the site of the bullet hole where a scar was taking shape. Finding Kira had left quite a few of those on both of us.

We were heading to John's to have dinner with him and Kira. Griff took a right, turning us toward downtown instead of staying straight on Forest Ave. to the interstate.

"Where are you going?"

"The office. There's something I want to show you."

We cruised Congress Street and took a right onto Temple to Middle. Griff slowed the car and pulled to the curb in front of the building that housed our office.

"What do you think of our new sign?"

A small white placard hung from an ornate rod iron post above the door. In old style black calligraphy it read, *Cole and Callahan, Private Investigators*.

My eyes filled, blurring the letters. "It's beautiful. I love it."

"The only change I'll ever make to that sign is when it needs to read, *Cole, Callahan and Sons.*

I laughed. "What if we have a daughter?"

"We'll name her Sam."

"It's just that simple?"

"It can be."

I'd proven my worth as a PI and earned my name on the sign by taking a lot of risks, albeit some stupid, but they'd paid off. Maybe it was time to take a few in my personal life too. I leaned across the seat and kissed Griff. Maybe he was right. Maybe it was just that simple.

Thirty minutes later, we pulled into John's driveway and stopped the car behind the black Suburban. Kira met us at the door. Though her face was still thin, you'd never know the hell she'd lived through from looking at her. Smiling in jeans and a turquoise sweater, her hair in a French braid, she looked like any other teenager. Only the wisdom in her eyes told us there was far more there than we could see.

John was on the back deck, flipping steaks on the grill. Only in Maine do people do outdoor grilling in forty-degree weather. You have to take it when you can get it.

"Wine and beer in the fridge," John said. "Help yourself."

Griff poured me a Chardonnay and took a Red Hook for himself. John raised his can of Diet Coke. "Cheers."

Over dinner inside, the conversation inevitably turned to the pending trial. Myles had joined Clive in Grand Falls and was being held and charged along with a myriad of others that the Bon Sejour raid had uncovered. LeBlanc couldn't have been happier with the outcome.

"Trial starts next month for Isaac," John said. "Stebbins will follow."

"Either of them talked?" Griff asked.

John shook his head. "They're too loyal or too stupid. Either way, neither of them will see the light of day for a very long time."

"I went to visit Ruth," Kira said.

All eyes fell on her, but I wasn't surprised. "How is she?" I asked.

"She was happy to see me."

I smiled. "You were important to her."

"If it hadn't been for Ruth mailing that postcard, I'd, I'd still…" she stopped.

John laid his hand over hers. "I'll make sure they know that at the trial. I don't think she'll fair too badly. She's been completely forthcoming. I'll do whatever I can for her."

I sipped my Chardonnay and looked out the picture window over the frozen lake thinking how easily fathers can build or destroy a daughter's sense of worth. Nurture a daughter's self-esteem and you get someone like Kira or Griff's daughter, Allie, survivors because they know they matter. Crush a daughter and you get Ruth or me, never quite good enough, but towing the line hoping someone will notice.

"….the real hero," John said. "Britt?"

"Sorry, what? I was admiring the lake."

"I said you were the real hero in all of this." John raised his glass.

"I didn't do anything but what I was told." I felt Griff's eyes on me and turned to look at him.

"Seems to me you did everything you weren't told. Like go to Isaac's in the first place, leave with Lucas, try to escape, give my phone number to the cop at Rusty's and last but not least, take down Lucas." I don't remember telling you to do any of those things."

Out of habit, I started to downplay my accomplishments, but then I realized he was right. I had done those things on my own. I couldn't quite see myself as a hero though, since each of those decisions had almost paralyzed me with fear and aren't heroes supposed to be fearless? But I raised my glass with the rest of them acknowledging that there had been a subtle shift along the fault line.

AUTHOR BIO

Patricia Hale received her MFA degree from Goddard College. Her essays have appeared in literary magazines and the anthology, My Heart's First Steps. Her debut novel, In the Shadow of Revenge, was published in 2013. The Church of the Holy Child is the first book in her PI series featuring the team of Griff Cole and Britt Callahan. Patricia is a member of Sister's in Crime, Mystery Writer's of America, NH Writer's Project and Maine Writer's and Publisher's Alliance. She lives in New Hampshire with her husband and two dogs.